OLD, PERSISTENT SPIRITS
SIX FANTASTICAL SHORT STORIES

PHILIP GLADWIN

For Shirley, who was curious about my backstory.

And the pool was filled with water out of sunlight,
And the lotos rose, quietly, quietly,
The surface glittered out of heart of light.

T. S. Eliot

CONTENTS

1. This Is The Wolf Run 1
2. The Ice Seed 16
3. Calenture 33
4. Indian Summer 47
5. Old, Persistent Spirits 56
6. In the Days of Increasing Automation 73
 Epilogue 89
 Do you write too? 96

1

THIS IS THE WOLF RUN

Something terrible happened to my brother. A long time ago, when I was still very young. The chaplain is kind. She wants me to remember. I'll try to piece it together. For her. Not for anyone else.

Late October. The sun is pale, and low in the sky. The nights are longer and colder; the soil turns to mud in the rain. The light of summer recedes.

If you're young, new to life, and susceptible, then you'll recognise the primitive dark of each evening. The night creatures you've read about are waking, in the shadows along the lane, in the odour of dankness under the trees, in the wailing of the wind. You're receptive in your fears, eager to believe —

— at the tea-table I snatch the shell from Patrick's eggcup. He grabs my arm and twists and I shriek in pain. I pull away, and we topple to the floor, wrestling for the eggshell. He sits on my chest to pin down my arms. I knee his back, and he pitches forward. I wriggle out from under him, and throw myself back on him, vision ragged with rage. We roll across the carpet, locked together, until my mother runs through from the kitchen and pulls us apart.

She understands and Patrick should, too. When he finishes his egg, he should turn the shell upside down and batter it through with his spoon. If you don't hole the shells, they get used by witches as sailing boats. I have dreams about great creaking vessels, rolling amidst heavy seas, heading towards me, sailing on over my head as I struggle to swim in the giant waves. High above, I see the dreadful face of the witch as she peers over the jagged edge of the giant shell, oblivious to me as I shrink into the water.

I forgive Patrick, for he is too strong to understand my fears. Today it is my ninth birthday. This morning his face was kind as he told me about the ceremony. He told me how there was good, dark soil beneath the church at the end of the garden, and how he and John would help me through the worst parts of the tunnel. I had to tilt my head back to see him speak, for he is tall, strong, and powerful. He is twelve years old, and invincible. He has many friends, but John is the oldest. He is fifteen, and his chest is thick like a man's. The muscles on his back tremble and the golden hairs on his forearms catch the sunlight as he climbs the apple tree. Last Saturday he told me about a family who spent the entire night trapped in their house by a yellow face which climbed the walls and looked in all the windows. The face was yellow like the new sickle moon; he said. It had a greedy smile and sharp teeth.

I keep remembering how it was still dark last Christmas morning when I woke. It was dark, but the streetlamp outside sent light through the curtains. Patrick knelt on the carpet. He was unwrapping a present. I watched long enough to see it was a book. I couldn't wait any longer and I pulled the first box from the top of my pillowcase. On the lid was a picture of Godzilla wrestling with King Kong. They looked like they were dancing the waltz. I held it out in joy.

'Look Patrick, a kit. We'll do this first!'

He smiled at me and nodded, holding out his book.

'You can have this, Davy. You'll like it.'

When my hand touched it, the cold of the book ran through my whole body. I looked at the cover. A beautiful woman with long dark hair held a crucifix with both hands. She looked scared. On her shoulder, rested on her shoulder by someone standing up behind her, was a hand with long, sharp fingernails. Each fingernail was creamy white, from the point to the cuticle. The letters that spelled 'Dracula' on the cover were red and awful.

Patrick read the entire book after me, and he was brave about it. But then he was the one who found the spaceship in Crow Holt. It was late one night, so late the night was turning into morning, and he and John were out exploring. They saw lights in the middle of the wood, and a strange noise like the elephant sound the Tardis makes. As they watched, the lights faded out, and the noises stopped. They said they ran to look, but the ship had gone. I couldn't believe their bravery, how like heroes they were, for they had already told me the story about the aliens who had landed in South America and left nothing of the Head Man of the village except for his skin, folded flat on a rock in the jungle.

Now it's me that needs bravery. It is half-past six, after tea, and I stand in the white-tiled bathroom. I wash my hands over and over again. The water is warm, and the soap I watched my mother put on the sink smells nice. But through the frostings on the window, I can see the shadows of the trees moving outside. They make a scratchy, repetitive pattern, black and the moon is cold silver.

Patrick and John are waiting for me at the end of the path. I have my wellingtons on, my grey shorts and my green anorak with the hood. Patrick is wearing his big duffel coat. He is holding a torch. The light from it shines upwards over his face as he speaks. He tells me not to worry. He tells me that all the boys have to do it when they are nine. He has done it. John has done it. Everyone I see at school who is in Miss Bucannon's class, and everyone who is older, has done it. They will take me to the tunnel mouth now, and they will meet me at the other end. The tunnel isn't long, but I must go quietly, because the monster will be awake and listening.

I let them push me forward. We go through the churchyard, almost halfway down to the lake, and we go into the bushes behind the church. We stop, and I see the mouth of the tunnel. It is dark, darker than the night around me. Patrick and John are talking to me, but I can't hear what they're saying. I stop listening. In front of me, the tunnel mouth opens wide. Darkness, drawing me, pulling me in. I think for a moment. I can picture how the monster sits and waits. He crouches, his bull head heavy. His eyes are blind, he doesn't move. He listens.

Patrick and John have told me about the monster. I know his name, and I know his weakness, and this will help me past him. I know he is called Stonefingers and that he has only one arm. I know that the other socket had the arm ripped from it many years since, but that the blood still escapes there. I know he is powerful, and deadly, and that he is hungry, and angry, but slow. If he blocks my passage, I am to run at him, and to run at that side of him where his arm has to stretch to reach me.

It is my ninth birthday, and I must grow into a man. I am resolute.

There is mud underfoot, but no water yet. The trees

close in on top of me as I walk. It gets darker as they cut off the moonlight, and then I know I'm in the tunnel.

It is not silent in here. I hear movements to my left, from behind me moving to my left. I stop to listen. I slip my hands into my pockets. It's hard to breathe. My fists are balls, my toes are curled. Standing there, head held alert, eyes wide, wide open, I listen for movements.

Stonefingers lives all the year round in a cave under the lake where his breath steams around him and there is perpetual frost on his fur. He comes every autumn to test the new boys, to take one or two back, to find his food for the winter.

There are no movements.

I walk forward, and stop for a moment, thinking of the church, the massive tower standing far above my head, and how the weight of its holy stones should have clamped the mouth of the tunnel shut. I step on. Our family doesn't go to church, and at this moment I wish we did. But my father doesn't care, and my mother says it's stupid, and the hymns make me yawn. Besides, would it make any difference? I ask God for help, and I try to pray to Jesus, but all I can think of are the evil bats that steal their homes under the rafters of God's church, how the stones of the church crumble at the corners of the walls, how the candle flames at the altar throw such a dim light into the nave.

As I lift my boots, each step that I take throws sound into the dark air of the tunnel. I can't see around me. Here it is dark, when our house is so light. At this moment, the fire is lit in the back where my mother and I sit in the evenings, the lights from the television illuminating our faces, playing on the ceiling, brightening the darkest corners of the room.

Thin water oozes under my feet. I catch my breath as I splash, far too loud. I am walking along the thin gutter that feeds into Stonefingers' lake. I am walking the path to Stonefingers' home. I stare to see, but there is nothing. All around me is black.

I think of my mother's face as she watches the television, and then I think of my family. How they try to help me. My father knows I am weak and frightened, and he spent a whole evening with me, talking to me, telling me things. He showed me book after book, saying how vampires aren't real, how they burned all the witches, how the spaceships are weather balloons and strange clouds. When he was with me, I felt his love, and I felt protected. But the next night he left me to myself, and my nightmares came back. My books don't help. The books and the films and the TV don't help at all. They make it worse.

I move on down the tunnel, and as I go, I repeat to myself how I do have the love of my mother, and my father, and most of all, I have the love of Patrick. To be with him, to be like him, I can do this.

I keep stepping forwards.

Light flashes ahead of me. A beam of yellow lances down the tunnel, searching for me. And I can hear Patrick's voice!

'Davy, this way! You're so close!'

I sob with a sudden relief. I drag my boots through the mud, not caring about the noise. I want to run —

— and there is Stonefingers. There, at the tunnel mouth, big against the light, is Stonefingers. He is huge, and he is growling. As his head swings from side to side, I know he searches for me, listening to pin me down. Yet I know he is slow, and blind, and that I must do it, so I run.

I dodge, he snarls—and they were wrong. Stonefingers has two arms. He moves like lightning, like a silver fish in the lake, and he has me! With his two massive fists, he clamps my wrists together. He bends closer, and I see the fur on his head, the cold white marble of his eyes, thick frost in each socket—and he pulls me to him.

Stonefingers opens his mouth. The revelation, the glistening blackness. His teeth are sharp and many, and the voice of his growling is ancient, deep, and murderous. As he pulls me in, I twist in his grip. Like mercury in a maze, I bend and slip. As he pulls me closer, I scream. I howl at him. He pulls at me, reeling my life in as my spirit leaves me in the wind from my mouth, in the snot dribbling from my nose, in the tears that run from my screwed-up eyes.

Then Patrick is shouting again. It's confusing. I can't understand it.

'Davy! Davy! Stop it! John!'

I hear him splashing through the water. He is coming into the tunnel. This can't happen. Patrick doesn't have to meet Stonefingers again. He will die because of me. And yet, for a moment, I want to call out to him, to urge him on to help me, to die with me, to be there with me at the time of death.

Stonefingers lets me go, and I turn, and I run back, running for my life. As I run, I notice things. That the tunnel has no roof, only tree branches, that the walls are only the elder plants and tall cow parsley of the churchyard.

I force my way back through the barbed wire fence, back into our garden, and I run out in front of the curtain of the willow tree. There is our back door with light pouring out, and my mother, calling for me.

'Davy? Davy? What's the matter? Where are you?'

I run to her, and throw myself at her, and as she holds me against her stomach and rocks me, I apologise for not being quick enough through. As I cry and scream and pour out my worthlessness, the bushes rustle behind me. She stiffens and stops stroking my neck, and I choke with new terror. But her voice is accusing, not fearful.

———

As I lie in bed, I can see spots of uneven plaster on the ceiling of my room. The nightlight points them out with hump-backed smudges of shadow. I know them all. There is a thin thread of spider web hanging from the beam by the window that has avoided being dusted for the entire summer. I know its shape like I believed I knew Patrick.

My mother showed me the wolf mask John had worn. Patrick cried in his bedroom later that night after father had come home. For a day, I was free.

Then night came again, and I remembered what it was like to run back through the tunnel in the darkness. I know that when the curtains moved a few minutes ago, I was safe; I have new window locks on all the frames. Patrick said that I shouldn't have them, that I was too stupid and that I deserved a real fright, but I made my mother get them for me and I tightened them shut myself until the key made white marks on the flesh of my fingers.

Patrick said that going through the tunnel would make me a man. This wasn't true. I am young, I am new to life, and I am weak. I remember how things looked. I saw the witches sitting up in the trees, and as I ran, I felt their soft hands draw through my hair. I remember how behind the elder plants there was the silver spaceman from that terrible film I watched with Patrick last Saturday night; and I am lost, even worse than before.

———

In the space of a day and a night, things change. Patrick and I go on. We live together, we get up each day, we eat our breakfast together—but it is different. I see him come out of the bathroom in the morning, his face red from the hot water and his hair sticking up, but the skin on his face still looks dirty. When John comes round after school, they go off together and ignore me. In the evenings, he does his homework, and we watch television. He comes and sits near me, on the settee, and I move away, onto the floor, to the other side of the room.

At night when we go to bed, I want to close my bedroom door, but I cannot. I must feel the light of the house on my face. Yet when the door is open, I can hear him there in the next room. He sleeps with his door open, and I hear him turn over in bed. I can hear the sighs he makes and the cries of his dreams; and I can hear his breathing. I hear his chest lift, and the flow of air past his teeth, across the red slab of his tongue, down the tubes of flesh into the centre of his body. He sucks on the world to breathe. I know biology, I see it on the television. I see how babies are born, shrieking and bloody, and I see how they die, returning to the blackness. I see all that life is in the films and the plays and the series on the television. I understand the world. I know what is happening. Evil is in our house. Evil has taken root and disguised itself. As I listen to him, I imagine what is happening. As the sound of his breathing swells and falls away, I see the pointed canine teeth growing, pushing back his lips. I hear the rustle as the snakes slip from his hair and the soft thump as they fall onto the floor, and the chirruping of the spiders that spill from his mouth to crawl into the warmth under the bedclothes.

I cannot bear it. I screw myself up, and pad along the landing to peer through the crack in the door at him. I am never quick or quiet enough to trap the signs before they retreat below the surface. I expect to see his face, dreadful, contorted, stationary, eyes wide open, staring at the ceiling, but he is always too quick for me.

I have not smiled at him again. I cannot. I avoid him. All the time I am sick inside, with metal on my tongue and bile in my throat.

Then, one evening when they are out and I watch television, there is the answer. There, in a film like all the rest, is the method laid out for me. I watch in terror as the slip into the abyss brings security for the ones who brave it. I understand the idea of allies, and we can use bad for good, and I see how to go forward.

The same night, in my bedroom, at the blue topped table in the window, I write my hatred on a scrap of paper —short, jagged runes, squashed close—and fold it small. I can't give it to him, but I go downstairs and slip it through a ragged seam in the pocket of his red jacket.

———

On the last day of sunshine before the winter we go out alone, the two of us. My mother sends us off. She gives us a picnic: sandwiches and cake in a plastic box, and some orange drink, and we put our boots on, and we go down the lane to the lake.

I sit on the jetty and watch him as he kicks around in the mud, struggling with the oars. I refuse to help as he drags the boat into the water. My mother had told me to fetch both our coats. I went round to the cloakroom and stopped. I could smell the washing powder from the machine. I was on my own. I put on my anorak and pulled up the zip. I listened for voices, but they were out at the front of the house, waiting for me. I raised my eyes from the floor, and I committed the greatest of treacheries. Instead of picking up his duffel coat, I reached to lift down his old red jacket.

At last, we set out, rowing out over the lake to the island. He talks, but I don't answer. He gets annoyed with me. I had brought the cricket set, and he had laughed at me, and told me it was the football season, but I didn't care. I wanted to play cricket.

Alone, the two of us. I sit in the stern and say nothing. As he rows, I watch the zigzags on his jumper, I watch the drops of water from the oars that land on his jeans, and I huddle, despite the sun, into my coat. I wait.

We land. We lay out the rug, put up the stumps and play cricket, and I see how bored he is. We eat our sandwiches and drink the orange in silence. I sit still, knees drawn up to my chin, and scan the sky.

He clambers up the slanting trunk of a fallen fir and crouches astride it near the top. He looks down at me. He's careful as he stands upright. He beats his chest with his fists and calls to me, expecting me to laugh.

'Hey Davy, Tarzan!'

Eventually, he points at the sun, low in the sky, and says it's time to go home. I hang back, waiting, watching the sky, and wondering. Then I see it. High above us, in a mass of indigo and purple clouds, I see the demon forming.

We launch the boat and start for home.

He says I should learn to row, so we stand up to swap places. As we cross over, I look up at his face. He is frowning, concentrating on keeping his balance. I rock my knees once and the boat sways. He squats and looks up at me, surprised.

'Davy!'

We both sit down, and I pick up the oars, beginning to row.

Out there, across the petrol-coloured surface of the lake, we can see trees and hills, but no houses, no people. There should be other boats, people fishing, but today we are alone. The valley of the lake is long and thin, running from north to south. It is not a big lake, but it is deep.

I row us away from the island, away from the cover of the trees, away into the middle of the passage. I cannot row properly; the oars are too heavy. I skim the surface of the water with one oar while the other digs itself in. I splash and we circle. Sometimes we move forwards, sometimes I shower us with fresh water.

He lies in the stem, watching me. I study the mud on his shoes, then I gaze at his jeans, then over his shoulders. I cannot look at his face.

Above us, in the black, rolling cloud, sweeping low across the skyline, the demon gathers.

Bored again, Patrick stands up and makes to exchange places.

I stand up too. We cross, and for a moment we both stand, facing each other. He looks down at me. I push him in the stomach as hard as I can. As he falls, he shouts, and he grabs my sleeves with his hands, looking at me in surprise. He leans backwards, clinging on to me and we sway there as the boat rocks. I panic, thinking it will over-balance us. His fingers slip along the nylon of my anorak, and he leans out even further. He releases a hand and tries to snatch a new hold, but I pull my arm back, and his fingers clutch and miss. I lean forwards to catch my balance as he falls. His other hand slithers along my sleeve, and then he is gone.

There is silence; then the demon falls on the boat.

His face is black and fiery and the air clashes in his wake. I cower in the bottom of the boat. I clench a cricket stump with both fists, and I kneel before his presence, his glory, and his darkness. I watch as he comes down on Patrick, and how Patrick's hands slip from the side of the boat under the pain of his blows, and I hear his voice as the demon pounds his body with hoof and fist and gathers the life from him. I shout to celebrate him; I shout as Patrick's eyes lock onto my own, as the cricket stump comes down upon his fingers, as the heavy wood smashes into his temple. He shouts and coughs, and swallows water, and his head dips again under the surface, and he surfaces only to choke again. I look him in the face as he thrashes, looking at his wide eyes as he grabs at the air, trying to block each blow; but the demon shows no compassion. I watch as he grows sodden with water, as he struggles more desperately, his body growing heavier. I see the strength of his arms leave him, how he stays under the water for longer each time, how he grows wracked in choking, and then how he stops.

Breathless, I crouch over the side of the boat. My hands grip the gunwale as Patrick slips away, as he turns face down, as he drifts out into the lake. I look up, away from him. Across the lake, the trees billow as a gust of wind blows over them. Clouds of leaves swirl down, then the wind passes. On the surface of the lake there is a great, pure silence.

I fall back into the bottom of the boat, shrieking with ecstasy and cold. Cartoon demons rush across the sky before my eyes. They have shiny red skin and pincer hands outstretched, and they are all fleeing from the greatest and darkest one; the demon I have summoned. I kick my feet and wriggle against the planks, pounding the wood with my fists, shouting until my head feels close to bursting.

After a long time, I look out over the bows of the boat, but I can see nothing. The daylight is going, and the surface of the water is grey. Leaning far out, I plunge my face beneath the surface of the cold water. I try to focus as I adjust to see underwater, then I pull back, screaming. His face had been inches from mine. I kneel for a minute, trembling, and then I lean back over the side and put my head under again, more slowly.

He hangs there under the surface, suspended in front of my eyes. I watch him swaying, turning over. I watch his hair drift across his face, covering his open eyes. I see his hands, his loose fingers, white in the pale green light, and how his arms hang. I see how the green weed at the bottom of the lake stretches upwards to grasp him and pull him down, and I see his clothes send tiny bubbles of air to the surface.

I pull myself up into the world again, gasping for breath, a shower of droplets spattering around me.

I am rescued from the boat, wet and crying, choking with grief, and carried home to my warm house; I am stripped, washed, and dried in front of the fire. My mother looks deep into my eyes, but I do not yield. I do not reveal how Patrick was taken. When I tell my parents about the storm, they look at each other. As I talk about the rain, and the cloud and the thunder out on the water, they look disturbed. I lower my head and I cry.

Almost noiselessly, I tell my mother how Patrick had been showing off in the boat, how he had stood astride, a foot on each gunwale, and how he had slipped backwards, and fallen, and not come up again. I tell her how the weed at the bottom must have grabbed him and held him for its own, and how I had taken the oars and tried to find him, but how the boat had only rowed in circles and how I had given up. How the wind had started and made me drift across the lake, but how I had kept on trying, until I was too cold.

I look up and see how her eyes are full of tears.

I remember how the evil left him at the time of death, how his eyes paled, how the light in them died. How his arms grew still, and his fingers relaxed, and how his face became beautiful again.

The doctor comes and gives me a tablet with some water. When they think I am asleep, they leave my bedroom, pulling the door shut behind them. The dark closes in on me like before. As I hover on the verge of sleep, I am sure the nightmares will come. Then, for the first time I can remember, the fear recedes. I know why. I made an ally among the soft calling shadows, and he came, and with him I destroyed an evil. Now I am as brave as Patrick was, and now I will sleep the fearless sleep of the strong.

The chaplain is kind, and her face is beautiful as she listens to my story, but it's a trick.

When she is sure I've finished, she talks to me. She says there is no need for me to carry all this. She speaks some nonsense about how there is someone else, someone far greater, who loves me and who can carry all my pain—I stop her dead. I don't know what she means; there is no pain.

She asks me if she can pray for me. I shake my head. I've no need. No need for Jesus, no need for anyone else. I'm strong in myself.

We sit for a while longer, but we don't talk. I'm happy. I know she has finished. The hour ends, the warder comes. He lets her out, and the door slams behind her.

Here I am, alone again. Safe again. All my life, there have been so many wolves. So many battles, but I've never lost one. Over fifty long years, I've beaten them all.

2

THE ICE SEED

Our father had a steamboat. He steered up and down the muddy river, trading between the settlements. He travelled under the yellow sky and the brown foliage, singing to the mudrunners and talking to himself, absorbed in the shifting coils of the river. In summer, in the quiet evenings, he would hole up under a beelbee tree, smoking endless pipes, legs dangling over the gunwale. In winter he fought, battling with the floods that came down from the mountains, sifting through the debris from storms far upriver where thunder and lightning blasted the camps and men huddled in the shelters. To my mind, everything in the world was his cargo; packs of machinery, crates of tools, carvings, pigs, and once the perfect ice-packed body of a young man. He would come off the water to drink with a friend and his family, but he never left sight of the river. At the sea, he would heave to where the water churned as it met the waves. He would light an orange lantern and wait, reading one of his old books, rocking on the tides in the coastal mists until his contact ship found him.

My sister is Venus, my name is Virgil. I know—I'm

sure—he loved what we meant to him, yet he insisted on names that would remind him of Earth, far, far distant, and he left us alone with our mother in our house that nestled in the side of the gigantic ruin. We played in the mornings in the drawing room, and we grew up together without him. We learned how to cook and write, how to keep the stove alight, how to carry tools. We loved him when he visited, but he came only rarely.

Venus, tall, thin, white skin and black hair, was the leader. I was the apprentice. She guarded me when we played in the forest. She was the soldier, and I was conquered; in boats she rowed, and I steered. Every day, she saved my life in a hundred ways. When I saw my first shankertooth slip its way upriver, I climbed on a branch to spy on it. The branch bent and I toppled in, but Venus had seen me. She swam out to rescue me and she pulled me in.

When she broke her arm and fell ill with fever, I pledged her all my toys and sat in tears by her bed until she was well again. In life she did, and I tried as hard as I could to do like.

Somehow, my father always knew. He had been there at each of our births, and he was there for the last one, when my mother died. He and Venus carried the two bodies up onto the roof of the ruin. Too young to help, they left me behind in the house. When I heard the noise of the creatures of the air coming down for her and her baby, I opened my door and ran to her room, where I fell sobbing across her bed.

It changed then. He tried to change with it. He extinguished the flames of the boiler and moored his boat to the jetty by our house. He came to live with us, to take our mother's place. He put on his oldest clothes, clenched his pipe between his teeth, and spent day after day with a paintbrush, curled around the gables, shinning up the veranda and hanging off the gutters, splashing his way around each side of the house, marking his way over the blistered boards with a fresh white tide. We played nearby and brought him beer when he asked for it. By the time he had finished, the house stood out, high and bright amongst the dun of the forest, and the worst was past.

My mother and Venus and I had been caretakers. Father stopped travelling and came off the river to take over my mother's work. We lived in the shade of a vast ruin, and we spent our days tending the shell of a dead civilisation; our bending wills and soft human flesh keeping the ancient stones upright. The walls we inhabited were old and vivid with time. There were crumbling windows and immaculate arches, there were funnels, silos, great stairs, and closed towers. Venus and I were happy to remain there in the years after our mother's death because she had told us, and we believed her, that to live by the ruin was to live in the aftermath of giants. Our father stayed with us because he had to. Time passed, and my memory of her grew vague.

It was a day in late spring. The dawn mist had burned off, and the ruins lay under a high sun, drawing on the heat of the afternoon, the stone hot to the touch. Venus and I were sweating, high in a turreted tower, cleaning the lichen from the stone and following a tracery as it wound its way about the wall. There was no roof, and the sun was burning our backs as we scraped. We had taken our shirts off long before, but the heat was getting worse.

I fell backwards with a sigh, sprawling on my elbows and closing my eyes. Venus said nothing, but carried on scraping, crouched over the corner. I watched as she worked. She had tied her hair back because of the heat, and a drop of sweat ran from under her ponytail and down the length of her sun-browned back. She hit her finger with her mallet and stood up in a fury of frustration, nursing her hand. Then she wiped her forehead and loosened her belt, stepping out of her shorts in silence. She picked up her tools and attacked the wall again in a rage. I watched in wonder as she hammered at the stone. I had seen my sister naked many times before, but this time I noticed the muscles in her thighs, how they were hard under the skin, how her body curved, and I saw the cords of tension in her arms.

She stopped again and stood back from the wall, casting about her. At the far end of the platform was a stone obelisk, perhaps thirty feet tall, made up of rounded tablets of stone stacked one on top of the other. It had always been there; it stood out on the skyline and had been part of my youngest impressions of the ruin. Venus walked up to it and put her shoulder to it for a moment, testing her strength. She bent down and rubbed the palms of her hands in the dust, then pushed again. I stood up in alarm as I realised what she was doing. Each muscle in her arms and her shoulder flexed. Her back was bent, her hair hanging in her face as she leaned forwards, feet apart, her hands spread. She strained, then gasped and stopped, her hands on her knees, her head down.

I came forward to confront her, but, unsure of myself, I said nothing. She made no sign of noticing me, and I watched in terror as she started again. She gave a sharp cry, and the needle of rock loosened and toppled forward. The stones that fell onto the platform where we were working made a dull noise; but most of them went over the edge of the platform, disappearing in silence, tumbling seventy feet before vanishing into the treetops.

She looked up at me, panting and retying her ponytail. She was smiling, her frustration relieved. I turned away in confusion, trying to understand what she had done. Then, blown to me on the wind, there was a sound confirming summer, and all worries were driven out of my head. From the river, I heard the chugging, thumping noise of an approaching boat. I sprang to my feet and followed Venus in rushing headlong to welcome the first trader of the year.

It was John Catt. He was from the South, and his accent was strange; thick and slow, surprisingly cultured, as though he had once led a very different life. Venus and I sparked memories within him; whenever he was with us, he would always want to talk about his childhood back on Earth. He told us about his home, about the soft blue in the sky and the green of the damp land, the people he had known and the cities. He was old now, but still strong. He carried fuel upriver, filling barrels in the old way from a tap on the side of the tank, heaving them on to his back and carrying them ashore himself. He brought our caretaker's wages from the city: medicine, clothes, new knives, books. We knew him of old and were glad to see him. He distributed our supplies, chivvied Venus and me to help our father, and eventually took his place in the rocking chair on the veranda, accepting the glass Venus made for him with a sigh of pleasure. We all sat round him and put our feet up. An honoured guest, he would stay for a day or two.

When we had heard all the news of the trade on the river, and of the famines and riots in the city, it was evening, and when we had lit the fire and roasted the pig and eaten and drunk, it was far into the night.

The embers of the fire were the only light in the room when John Catt leaned over to me.

'Virgil?'

My father was asleep in his chair, one of his boots kicked off, his glass aslant in his lap. Venus lay face down on the boards in front of the fire. The room was very quiet.

'Virgil. How long have we known each other?'.

I answered, 'Years.'

'You trust me?'

I nodded.

'How old are you now?'

I thought for a minute. 'Fifteen.'

He looked at me carefully, counting. He looked at my father for a long moment and decided. 'Old enough then.'

He held his fist out to me. I watched him, half asleep.

'Look.'

He turned his hand round and spread the fingers one by one. I watched, puzzled. Then I pulled my head back. In the centre of his palm, I could see dust motes spinning and climbing upwards like smoke. I focused harder. The cloud thickened. I darted a look at his face. It was half in shadow, but I could see that he wasn't smiling.

'Look harder.'

A tiny flame, no bigger than a joint on my finger, jumped up at the centre of the cloud and burned with a pale light. It strengthened and grew taller.

I looked around. My father lay in his chair as he was, his mouth open and his chest rising and falling. Venus had brought her arms round above her head, the palms flat on the floor. I wondered if she was really asleep.

'Virgil, what do you want?'

I looked at him.

'Would you like a bird? Virgil?'

On his outstretched hand, at the centre of the flame, appeared an outline. It hardened, growing more substantial; bill, feathers and long tail appearing like a parrot of the forest. John Catt closed his fingers over it, and held them for a moment, then opened them wide. Lying flat on his palm was a tiny golden bird. He held it out to me.

'Take it. You can keep it if you want it.'

I reached out. It was solid, and heavy in my hand.

'Do you like it? You could do that if you wanted.'

He smiled at my confusion, waiting for me to say words that wouldn't come. I struggled, but the whisky had silenced me. At last, he settled back in his chair again, gazing at the coals in the grate.

'I was like you—a pale-skinned boy with sea-green eyes. I travelled a long way, sweating in the sun, working in the lands by the ocean. The insides of my arms were just like yours, white and blue veined, lined like a map.'

He stopped, and his head fell forward a fraction. The fire spat and a log shifted. His voice was thicker.

'I was too hot for it, too violent. So, they sent me here.'

I waited, but he was silent, and his eyes flickered. I realised he was very drunk. The moment was slipping past me. A headache crashed into my skull. My mouth worked, and I formed words.

'How did you do that? With the flame?'

He ignored me, but his eyes had flicked open again.

'Do you know who I think built these ruins?'

Numb, I shook my head. He gauged the look on my face.

'We did. Humans, on our first colonising round, not this time. We decayed, and moved on, over and over, until we stumbled across our own remains without knowing. It's as simple as...'

He saw he had lost me. 'We're a restless people. We wander to no point. We're temporary, rootless; the worst thing we could have done was discover star travel.'

My eyelids felt heavy. John's voice receded.

'...the chance to find our place, to be fixed like a jewel

in a necklace, vibrating in tune with the universe like an atom in a crystal. On this planet it's possible, but no-one will do it. We carry on with our old habits, not wanting to grow into our next phase. We always move on, drifting off like fragments of weed on the edge of the tide. We pass this way and that over the surface of the galaxy, we spread out, neither too close nor too distant, and we live, not knowing why.'

My father stirred in his seat, knocking his glass off his lap. It rolled down his legs and fell to the boards. I watched it spin, wondering why it had not broken. My father was waking up. He brought one hand up to his head and grunted.

John grabbed my arm and pulled me forward. His voice was quiet, yet urgent. His breath was strong in my face, and I felt queasy.

'Bind yourself into it. When you hear the bird that talks, listen. They unlocked it with their science, without knowing it, and it scared them and with a thousand rationalisations they moved on, drifted past. Not knowing why. Looking for somewhere they could belong. Not knowing what they had discovered here. Ask Venus.'

Venus rolled over onto her side. She opened her eyes and stared at the fire. Her face was immobile, inscrutable. John looked her up and down, appraising, then resumed, his voice different. Louder, clearer, more familiar, more public. I felt tired, and very sick.

'Did you know, Virgil, that we humans have never found advanced life anywhere? We've found all sorts, all across the galaxy, but we've never found companionship, we've never found a mirror. How lonely does that make us? There are primitive peoples, but there's no race more advanced. Where are they, Virgil?'

Something melted inside me. I lurched to my feet and

stumbled out down the corridor. I pushed the door to the toilet open, and I threw up into the pan, heaving until I was dry.

When I returned to the room, there was a tension. Venus had gone and my father and John were sitting upright in their chairs, staring at each other. My father spoke without taking his eyes off John.

'Virgil, don't drink so much if you can't take it. Go to bed.'

As I climbed the stairs, I could hear my father's voice, raised in anger. I clutched the banister with a hammering nausea in my head, straining to catch the sense of their argument. My father was demanding that John should leave us both alone. That something I couldn't understand, some fearful joint exploration of theirs, was over, had finished years ago, before Venus and I were even born, and should be forgotten. Then sickness overcame me again, and I staggered into my room.

When I woke, I was in my bed, and the sun was high in the sky over the house. I felt guilty, without knowing why. A pang of self-disgust made me uneasy. I lay there, listening for the noises that signalled we were on holiday, yet there was silence. I went downstairs, through the empty house. I slipped through the room where we had drunk the night before, skirting my father's chair, and stepping outside onto the veranda. It was hot outside. The sun blazed down on the trees, and the water of the river ran with white reflection. The mooring was empty. John Catt had gone.

My father was waiting for me inside. I smiled, ingratiating, but he didn't move, continuing to stare at me. I shut my eyes for a moment, my stomach turning again with nausea. I had rarely seen him this angry. I wanted to run away, but his question surprised me.

'Where's Venus?'

There was silence between us.

'I don't know.'

'Virgil, will you promise me something?'

I nodded, vulnerable.

'Forget what John Catt said.'

I looked at him. How could I make myself forget something? It was a stupid thing to ask; but he looked at me, and his eyes were hard, and then I was crying. He didn't move, but as I cried, he seemed to sink into himself.

Later, when I was sniffing, he came over and put his arm around my shoulders.

'Virgil, I trusted John Catt, and I shouldn't have. Venus is too young; she's never known men. Now you must help me. We have to find her.'

My father sent me along the bank of the river while he pushed through the trees and the undergrowth a few minutes into the wood. I looked from the water to the tree-tops, and back again. We had walked a mile, and soon we would come to our old tree house, where I thought she might be. When I arrived there, I was to shout, and wait for my father to come down to the water's edge. I didn't know what we would do then.

Then I saw John Catt's boat. It was moored in the shade, half hidden under the wide arms of a great leeman tree. I didn't call my father; I don't know why. Instead, I bent down and looked through each of the portholes. I couldn't see anyone inside. I climbed aboard and walked the length of the deck. No-one called out, no-one shouted. I opened the door and, turning backwards, climbed down the ladder into the half dark cabin. It was a room familiar from all those afternoons when John Catt had let Venus and me play aboard while he and my father sat and drank whisky. But this time there was a difference. A sense of imminence permeated the layers of dust and the wood of the table, and the nicotine-stained paintings on the curving roof seemed to move, on the verge of life.

I waited, for something. John Catt's parrot fussed and clicked, and the cage swung. Sunlight from a porthole lit an old enamel mug lying on a plate. Then it came. There was a flickering, a dislocation. A loudness, rising from nowhere. The parrot, its head cocked, scrutinised me with its eye. The ceiling faded away. Above me, between my head and the sky, a great distance—a tunnel?—with a silent, welcoming presence at the very end of it. I knew I was aware of those who had once built the ruin—and they were aware of me.

The bird cawed, and I took a step backward. I turned round and round—the room was silent. Pure silence.

Back outside I jumped to the bank and called my father. He came at a run, stopping when he saw the boat. The rage in his eyes made me scared again, and I told him nothing of what had happened. We spread out to restart our search, but this time it was not for long. My father met John Catt, walking back to his boat. I heard the shouts, and slipped past my father as he fought him, and ran into the trees where he pointed me, and crawled under a lip of rock into a cave I had known nothing about.

I stood up, careful of the low cave roof. In here I could hear nothing of the struggle outside. The air was cool and dank.

I couldn't believe what I could see. The remnants of Venus's secret life littered the sandy floor of the cave. Rotten food, books, pieces of fabric; paint spattered patterns across the rock of the walls. There was a low table with a row of candles across it. Venus lay in the corner, curled up in a mass of blankets. I couldn't see her eyes. She was naked, her clothes strewn around the makeshift bed. I looked around in sadness as my eyes grew accustomed to the low light.

I startled her when I woke her. I told her what was happening and helped her dress. We left the cave and headed back to the house. The path was empty apart from us. I expected Venus to cry, but she said nothing. My father came in soon after me, grey and cold-eyed. He wouldn't say where he had been.

That night their shouting kept me awake. He accused her, she cried and screamed. I pulled my pillow around my head, I counted aloud, I sang to myself, I banged my head with my fists to shut it out. Then, when the heat and the night seemed thick and suffocating, the shouting grew too close. I left my room but there was no-one on the landing. I went downstairs and saw my father outside, beyond the veranda. I opened the doors, and stepped outside, and saw that he was staring at the roof of the house, where Venus was crouching at the very peak of the high roof. She stood upright, and I held my breath as she spread her arms. We both watched as she turned her head skyward, and I flinched as the sound of her cursing came down to me. Then she walked off the end of the roof.

She fell in silence, drawing her body in, pulling her right knee up to her chest, turning in the air. As she hit the ground, she seemed to pull her head, looking away from us, or looking away from the ground, I'm not sure.

In the weeks after the accident, as I began to call it, I tried to talk to my father. He spent the time drunk, hunched in his chair by the grate, smoking. I talked at him for hours, and once, not showing that he was aware of me, he spoke about my mother, and how she could have prevented all this. Venus had told him she and John Catt had been together for three years. She said she loved him; my father had told her she didn't know what love was. And she said that now she never would. She said that John Catt had tried her with the magic, tried to awaken it in her, but she failed somehow.

I stopped listening to him after a while. It was rambling, regretful stuff, full of self-pity.

He stopped shaving, and his lined face became covered with stubble that thickened day by day into a ragged beard. He stopped washing, and he began to smell; a thin, unpleasant, acid smell that filled the room, and reminded me of his failure. As it became clear that Venus would live despite it all, I lost interest in him and shifted attention to the remains of my sister. I asked her questions. I was having visions, needs. On John Catt's boat, I had heard a greater life calling, and she knew something that she hadn't told me. Sometimes I imagined I found things in the ruins. Secret passages. Old writings. Cellars with old, locked boxes that fell apart and were empty. Old fragile weapons. Other times I had a glimpse, a taste, a scent of something indescribable, like a glowing centre in the darkness, or half glimpsed marble hallways.

I would rage about the room, Venus watching me, her head lolling but her eyes fixed on me. I wanted to know why she went bad, and why she did it, but she couldn't, and wouldn't, tell me.

A week ago, driven by the visions that were more and more frequent, I went into the forest. I carried a sack with me. It bumped between my legs as I ran. I went back to the bend of the river where John Catt's boat lay on its side in the mud, and beyond. I penetrated further into the trees, not caring where I was going, driven by a force I didn't understand, until I had come to a place I didn't know. It was a place where there were small ravines, rocky over-hangs, strange fissures and cracks in the rocks, a place where the trees were thick, yet growing wiry and stunted. I moved to the very edge of the deepest ravine, and climbed down, perhaps thirty feet. Then I found a deep overhang, a rocky lip more properly, the opening to a shallow cave. I stopped then and looked around.

Under the ledge, all was quiet. I moved to the back of the overhang, where the walls of rock formed a chamber about me. I squatted and looked out across the ravine. The closeness of the wall opposite and the forest above my head enveloped me, and I felt calmer, safe in my own secret cave. The light under the lip of rock faded as the sun set behind the trees opposite, and I watched the ravine grow darker. When I felt quiet enough, I lit my lantern, turning it down low to cast only dim illumination around me. The walls jumped into relief, yet the night hung across the mouth of the cave like a thick curtain, and I felt hidden.

I knew the shape of the ritual; the visions had made it clear. Like Venus must have done before me, I had fasted for days. I untied the draw string of my bag and pulled out a blanket of feathers I had sewn. I laid it down and contemplated the texture and the colours of all the birds. I pulled out the skins of the five rabbits I had killed, and a pouch containing needle and fishing twine. I sewed a hat, tall and thin, stiffened by the sticks. I pulled out a handful of the brighter feathers from the blanket and bound them into the seams of the hat, and then added leaves and moss that I found on the floor of the cave.

Then, slowly, slowly, I submerged myself. I poured water from my bottle on the soil and smeared the wet earth across my face. I wrapped the blanket around my shoulders. I put Venus' chain around my neck and opened the locket. I looked at the image of my mother held inside and then let the locket fall back open against my chest. I opened my scissors, and laid them in front of me, and smashed my mirror with a stone, and placed each shard on a rock or a ledge around the cave. Picking up the hat, I sat cross-legged in the centre of the room I had made, surrounded by a hundred reflections and cross images of the lantern, facing outwards into the night. I placed the hat on my head with both hands, waited for the glowing centre to approach me.

The lantern guttered, and the darkness closed in and supported me. I slept there, and I dreamed. My father and I were back in Venus' secret cave, and it was as before, except for the thing that moved over Venus' breasts as she lay on the bed; a thing of flesh and sinew, and black hair, crawling lower, towards the dark triangle at the base of her stomach. I tried to shout, to warn her, but could only groan. I tried to step forward towards her, but my feet were held. My father threw the stick he was holding, and we watched it as it spun off, turning end over end, to crash into the wall over the chair. The noise it made echoed and reverberated, and the thing scuttled off Venus, falling to the floor, racing into the shadows at the back of the room.

Thankful we had saved her, I moved to cover her naked body over with her shirt as I had done in real life, but I stopped in horror. Her lips were wet, and her eyes were half closed in pleasure. She seemed to be in a trance. As I stood over her, she refocused and fixed me in a stare of rage; her face contorting in hatred and disappointment, as she realised how we had frustrated her. Between us, my father and I picked her up, held her tight, and carried her to the safety of our house again. In the dream, I knew how wrong this was.

There is something very close now, another realm of non-corporeal life. Two days ago, I produced a gold bar— it spasmed out into the air in front of me as I walked to the ruin. It was real enough; heavy and dull. I left it on a rock in the sun. Although I am ashamed of how this betrayed a crass desire which I thought I had left behind, it shows how I am learning.

The bird that talks. Material powers, powers of the earth – and what after that? After years of trying, John Catt found someone who could walk this path for him. Meanwhile, my father lives still, alone, a husk. He stirs from his bed every day and goes to sit in the corner of the covered room in the ruin. He smokes, pipe after pipe; he too never speaks. Like a beetle in its nest, if beetles ever have nests. That knowledge has gone for me now. I'm beginning to know the rest.

It is too late now—that which he feared is done. The process is started in me. Venus is immobile, she lies there, her black eyes the only thing with life, staring at me with an emotion I cannot recognise—fear or envy, not apathy, I'm sure. I can only guess how she felt when John Catt abandoned her for me, and she felt the pointless claustrophobia that he had promised to lift settle again.

This morning I raised my glance from the jungle floor and found I could look down the river to the sea, all the way to the sea, and the city. This was not a dream. This was a new sense, a new way of being; this was hard experience.

I stretched my fresh sight, testing my new ability, until I could see the individual streets and dwellings. There are a million people in this city alone, and I could feel the impress of their lives. The young, playing in the sun, burning their limitless energy; the workers and the fighters, and the mothers and the drunks; and the very old, motionless, sitting in the cool shadow of trees, hoping their deaths would be sweet. Every one of them adrift, each one of them alone.

I can change this. I am the vanguard of our human migration. My control over the material world is growing, and soon I will stop electricity working. Then people will be stationary. Then, like a chain reaction, like a seed of ice crystallising cold water, this process can spread.

I, through no merit of my own, mysteriously, am the seed.

3
CALENTURE

'Hey, Rocket John, listen to this:

Power beyond belief, power to fuse and create. White plumes of smoke; brilliant light and shattering noise. Gus Ryland, strapped in a seat in a silver ship pointed at the sky, his face distorting, the flesh on his bones sucking and twisting as the earth groaned and the sky cracked open and the ship hauled itself into the black. His eyes the only constant in that mess of energy; fixed on a rigid point impossibly far beyond the screen that flickered in front of his face.

See—they're all talking about you!'

Olivia finished reading aloud and slammed the fat paperback down onto the table in front of him. 'Why is it that every single book I pick up is for children? Full of rockets and macho men! Stupid men in stupid macho space suits!'

He stared at her, wondered how he could look at her, and love her, want her more than ever; and yet despise her at the same time. This was new.

He wondered what he could say, what would please her. Until she tired of waiting for a reaction.

'Oh, John, please. I don't have the energy. What's

wrong with you these days? All this leave you've been in a daze. Since that last trip. What's going on?'

She wanted to talk to him about leaving his job, about how she never wanted him to fly a freight ship again, about how, if she meant anything to him, he would leave the supply runs to those people with no family, with nothing to lose, who... She couldn't finish her sentence, but he knew what she meant: people who could die hurting no one else. He had no words. Something had happened the last time he flew that meant he couldn't answer.

'Oh, man!'

She gave up, yielding to something obscure. She looked down at her watch, her mood opaque.

'Where's Harper?'

She got up, picking up her bag and going to the door.

'Get ready, will you? You two are as bad as each other.'

He watched the door swinging closed behind her, listening first to her footsteps as they died away, and then to the splashing of the fountain in the square. It was midday, and although he hadn't been outside yet, he knew how the Provençal sky would be shining brilliant blue, how the sun would be pouring down onto the melon-fields and the winding streets and the courtyards of the village.

There in the room where he preferred to wait, it was almost dark. In these ancient houses, the windows were small and the walls thick. Outside, the leaves of the trees soaked up the light that trickled into the canyon of the narrow street between the houses. It was silent now; only the flies to irritate him as they circled and darted, crawling among the drops of honey and the crumbs on the table-cloth, and spiralling above among the strands of beads and glass dangling from the lampshade.

Harper came downstairs, her sandals clattering on the stone slabs. She brushed through the fringed curtain at the foot of the stairwell and came to the front part of the room, standing by the front door and looking into the mirror on the wooden dresser that was cluttered with bottles, candles, books, and sardine tins. She stood combing her hair, her back to him, saying nothing, but he saw her face in the mirror, as she grimaced in annoyance at the knots.

Olivia reappeared at the doorway, counting the notes in her purse, and looking impatient. The scene forced itself on his mind. The soft browns and greys of the old room glowed in the noon dusk. Gold and soft, polished bronze, lambent in the muted light from the street. Emotion exploded in him—the girl at the mirror could have been anyone; the three of them any three people who had lived together for forty years or more in that village. He felt the bonds between them strengthen as the names and the pasts melted, and, for a moment, he felt a part of the two women. He held the stolen moment of belonging close to him.

Olivia found more money. They drove to Aix and wandered around the wide avenues. They had ice-cream, they watched the students in the cafés, they wondered what to do, and they argued. The day didn't work. Harper was bad-tempered and aggressive; Olivia was sullen and withdrawn. John got angry, with himself more than anyone, as coldness descended again. With some desperation, he pointed out a poster for an exhibition at the museum, regretting this when it gave Olivia space to vent her bitterness with him.

'You're just a driver, aren't you? You're not interested in things like this.'

She was right, of course. In the museum he was restless, uninvolved in the art, watching Harper and Olivia as much as the paintings. At one point, he found himself standing behind them as they stood, shoulder to shoulder, both looking up at a pencil sketch, both clasping their hands in front of them. Their similarities reminded him they were twins. Not identical; they usually appeared quite dissimilar, but at that moment John couldn't tell them apart. Their hair was the same colour and texture, but one of them did not brush it, so it always hung in a slight tangle. He used to know who that was, and he would remember if he tried, but for the moment he let it confuse him. They wore similar clothes—light blouses and unfashionably long skirts with sandals. The folds in the loose clothes hid the difference in their bodies, normally an easy way of telling them apart. The illusion was complete; they seemed indistinguishable. How was he to fix the associations and memories due to each when they stood like this?

His affection foundered, bewildered. He moved forwards, looking to decide which one was Olivia. Satisfied he knew, he relaxed, and the strange moment was over. He rested his hand on her hip, lifting his gaze to the picture above them. When Harper smiled up at him, her forehead wrinkled in surprise, and Olivia turned round, and he knew he was wrong, the shock dragged the pleasant confusion back over his head. He was lost, swimming under water, the light receding above him.

Much later they drove back, sitting in the car in a peaceful quietness, happy together again, the light blazing across the fields as the sun neared the hilltops, the heat ebbing a little at last. Harper went to buy food for the dinner, and when he and Olivia were alone in the house, before he put the lights on, he turned to embrace her. She kissed him and seemed happy. He felt alive and energetic, that the day had been a success after all. He stared into her eyes and thought he knew the truth. Carried along by the warmth of the emotion, his lips formed the question; but at that second her face blanked in warning. He caught himself, but it was too late. She pulled away, her eyes narrow, her face closed. After a moment's silence, she shrugged and pushed past him. He looked after her, then sat down at the table.

When Harper came back with the sausages and the wine, Olivia opened the first bottle and they cooked. They finished the bottle and opened a second, and John concentrated on the food and forgot his rejection.

Their guest, Manou, arrived, bursting in, licking his lips, insisting that he had pursued the delicious aromas blindfold from the very edge of the village. He brandished his bottle of wine, kissed them all twice, and began to talk about the affairs of the village.

They sat down to eat. Manou was a friend of the twins. They had been taking their holiday in this village for fifteen years, first with their parents and then on their own, and John could have been jealous of the familiarity the other man had with the two of them. Yet it was impossible to take against him—with his round, wire-framed glasses, the thin, waxed moustache he wore so unselfconsciously, and the constant stream of jokes he told so self-effacingly, he seemed to embody likeability.

That night, however, towards the end of the main course, Manou allowed his mood to falter. He talked about a good friend of his who had been murdered some weeks before. He grew more emotional as he told the story. His friend had been having an affair with a married woman who lived in a house out in the country. One night, when he had taken Manou over to meet her, her husband arrived home, carrying a shotgun. At gunpoint, he told Manou to leave, and Manou had driven straight to the police station. When he and the police returned to the house, it was all done. The man had killed Manou's friend, and the woman, and then turned the gun on himself. He had failed to kill himself, and had been arrested, and would be standing trial soon. Manou told the story, sniffing, and they listened, and watched as his eyes sprouted tears.

'Such a terrible ending. And to think,' he finished, loudly blowing his nose, 'it was all because of Love. A man, and a woman, together—it should be happy until the end. But life is always too muddled.'

Mournful, he stared at the fruit bowl. Harper brought through the pudding, and John opened another bottle, and Olivia stroked Manou's hand, and the evening recovered. They smoked, and Harper lit a candle, and then Manou wanted to go out to see the sky. The nights in August were warm and the countryside inviting, so they walked up the hill behind the church and sat on the ancient tombs to look at the stars.

The conversation slowed, and they contemplated the stream of brilliance that poured across the sky. A companionable silence came between them, and John relaxed. He wondered why the black of space became such a warm blue blanket with the earth behind him. His mind blurred by the drink, he slipped down off the tomb to lie on the tough bladed grass, still getting a faint thrill from the experience. He had grown up in a city, and the first time he had been away was when he was seven and the staff took him and all the children in the home on a trip into the country. After what seemed like an endless drive, they ended up at a big old mansion, lying deep in massive, untended grounds. To John, used to the claustrophobias and the proximities of the city's housing projects, the space around the house seemed wonderful, unbelievable.

He remembered what he did that afternoon, over twenty years before. They played in the garden and, while all the other children were running around and soaking each other with water, shrieking in the sun, he wandered far from the house until he found a huge, sprawling rhododendron bush. He crawled into the very centre of its tangle and squatted there, his knees against his chin, the unfamiliar dust from the branches and leaves winding about him, tickling his throat, and making him want to sneeze. He felt the hands of the bush press against him as he leaned his head against the bark, the texture strange against the shaved skin of his scalp. The insects crawled on the leaves, and, as time passed, birds returned to the trees above him. He waited there for the entire afternoon, enclosed and buoyed up by strip after strip, layer after layer of tiny life.

He thought about that afternoon, incredulous at how quickly life was passing. He wondered at the expanse of time that separated him from that small boy. He realised how much he had changed. Even this once-comforting memory now produced an overwhelming claustrophobia.

Manou broke the silence, jolting him away from the past.

'You are a starman, Johnny. What is up there?'

John focused his thoughts.

'Oh ... a load of ... nothing.'

That wasn't enough for Manou. John tried to be precise.

'Cold. Blackness. Thought, perhaps.'

Manou got up and walked to the far edge of the hill, looking out over the fifty-foot drop to the valley floor. He spoke quietly, without turning his head.

'It sounds very lonely.'

John didn't answer. It had come out wrongly. That wasn't all of it.

Harper asked the next question.

'So why do you do it?'

He didn't answer, for he was angry. How like Harper, to ask the question she knew would cause an argument. He loved flying the supply ships; he had spent time on the lunar passenger service, and the rough edges and the hardness of the run to the Ceres installation only enhanced the thrill of leaving the atmosphere, when the Earth shrank behind, and the region of the absolute pushed itself against him. Yet at that moment, drunk as he was, with the stars so bright above him, he agreed with. He wondered how it was possible to be enveloped by nothing.

He sat up and looked around him, confused. Manou spoke again.

'It's very dangerous, I believe. Many men die—and the isolation on the trip must be affecting?' He waited, but John said nothing. 'You know, I heard once about sailors, sailors on the sea, in the old times—in the real old times, when they had wooden sailing ships. A fever called the Calenture affected them. You have heard of this, John?'

His voice was soft in the dark, but John sensed an approaching discomfort.

'When the sailors were out in the middle of the Atlantic, or the Pacific, and it was hot, and they were a long way from land, and they hadn't seen their lovers for months, and months, then they would go crazy. They would burn with the desire to throw themselves into the sea. And some of them would do it. Nobody knows why. Some people said it was because they hallucinated in the heat and thought that the sea was the green fields of their homeland. I think that this is stupid. They were only sailors, only men, and no doubt dirty after all that time on board ship. Of course they would want to immerse themselves in that immense, rolling, cool expanse of water. Of course they would. And those that experienced the Calenture, but swam, and survived and—well, once they felt it, they never forgot it, you know. How could anyone forget that impression of peace? I even think that some of them were addicts; they would endure all the filth and poverty and the hard labour of life on ship just to feel that sensation again. Don't you agree, Johnny?'

There was a long silence, and John realised that Olivia and Harper were waiting for him to answer. He shook his head; he was drunk, and furious. Then Manou chuckled.

'No, I know why you do the space-flying. You hope to see God.'

Olivia snorted, and John smiled, relieved despite himself.

'I've not met God. In fact, no-one so far. But I fly the day after tomorrow, and I'll have a look for you. Have you any messages for Him, Manou? Any requests?'

Manou shrugged his shoulders, and threw a stone down the cliff, silent again, his body a black outline in the dark.

Harper and Manou went back to the house soon afterwards, leaving Olivia and John alone together. When the sound of their voices had died away, she slipped off the tombstone and lay down next to him. She put her arm across him, and he relaxed again; this rare affection surprised him. Yet as he held his body still to stop her moving, his mind drifted back into a region that seemed white and still. He lay in peace, drawing a strength from the starlight and the cold radiance shed by the old moon as it crouched above the horizon.

'Johnny, what happened on your last trip? Something bad, I know.'

She waited. Gave it one last try.

'Why don't you give it up? Come back to earth. Get a normal job.'

He grunted something and pulled her closer to him.

He hadn't told her about his last trip, and he never would. It had been a disaster. The computer failed when he was barely out of orbit, sending the ship across the sky in leaping cartwheels. He took override, for the first time since training school, and burnt the small reserves of fuel for the docking manoeuvres in trying to regain control. He made it back down to a stable orbit, with the Earth visible as a slim crescent of light in the corner of the single port-hole, but it was a long wait until the rescue shuttle picked him up. It had been hard. The air server stopped with the computer and, close to suffocating, he grew delirious.

He thought back. He hadn't been too scared, but there was something else, something more significant about the situation. He kissed the top of Olivia's head and tried to clarify his thoughts.

It was to do with the fact that he could only see a frag-ment of the earth through the porthole. If he was in any danger of dying at all, he would have liked the opportunity of seeing the swirling blue mass that lay so tantalising around the corner of his vision. Being forced to concen-trate on the edge disturbed him so much. He knew the Earth reached out with its air and its gravity in a dimin-ishing grasp, but from where he was sitting, the edge of the Earth seemed too abrupt, too sharp—one step into clean blackness.

As the air became more stifling, and after he finished trying to breathe activity into the computer, he gave up cursing and wasting time. He settled back into the webbing cradle and tilted it to see the viewport without moving his head. He agreed with Olivia when she called him a driver. The point about dying now, eighty years after the initial steps to the moon, was that a death in space was worth no more than a comparable accident on Earth. John wasn't born when the first disasters of the

Soviet and the American space programs had created the heroes whose names he could still reel off, but in a museum in Paris he had seen the library footage of the Challenger explosion. Though he was very young, and didn't understand death, or what the men and women in the shuttle were trying to do, he had been deeply impacted.

Of all the exhibits in the museum, it was this flickering video that held him for hours, and years. He remembered how the ship tore open the soft black of the sky, then halt, and fragment, and be squandered. He thought of himself, a boy among millions going past the exhibit, and again he remembered the glory and the imagination that had pushed him into a ship that burst from the planet into the cold of space.

As the temperature rose in the cockpit, he grew feverish, slipping into a dream-filled state. The sliver of the Earth became the focus of his attention. Or rather, the edge of the silver-blue crescent; the line at which it stopped and where sterility began. Pure contrast, for even the light of the stars, although energy and vigour, did not guarantee the teeming of life as did the blue of the Earth. There, in front of him, was the division between life and confusion, and the Absolute.

He had grown delirious, wondering what he looked like from outside. The thing about the porthole was that it was sometimes easy to imagine something looking in. But, hard as he tried, he couldn't see where the person outside would stand to get a clear view of the inside. The moon was a long way off and after all, it would get chilly holding a telescope out in the open there. And after the moon, that lump of sterile rock, there were no footholds until the asteroids —and if you missed them then ... Imagine falling that incredible distance, and the blankness, and the absence.

Once in a hundred years a fragment of rock, once in a millennium the minute tangle of the bubbles of life...

He woke up on the hillside, sweating from the nightmare. Olivia slept next to him. He stood up, stiff. He looked at his watch and turned to the southeast. There, in the distance towards Marseilles, on time as usual, rose a burning light that flared a moment as it climbed, then was lost among the stars.

He woke Olivia up, and helped her up, holding on to her as she overbalanced into his arms. He put his arm round her and they walked back to the house where he intended to keep her talking till dawn. He had one day left; Harper would be asleep by now, and John enjoyed having Olivia to himself.

'Will you marry me?'

While Harper was opening the boot of the car, he forced himself to ask Olivia. She didn't answer; he tried to hold her. Her seat belt got in the way, and when he made to undo it, she stopped him, putting her hand on his for a second.

'John, you're late already.'

He looked away from her, amazed at the tears pressing in his eyes, and climbed out of the car. Harper came round to his side, and she took the keys from him. She walked with him halfway toward the gatehouse, then stopped him. He realised her hand was on his arm.

'I don't want to intrude or anything, but—'

'Go on.'

'You know she'd marry you if you stopped flying?'

He sighed, angry again. 'Yes.'

'And if you don't, it's over?'

'Yes.'

'So will you?'

'I can't.'

'I thought not. Oh well, take care Johnny.'

The softness in her tone startled him. He turned and saw how she gazed at him.

'But listen,' she said. 'I think it's cool. The flying.'

She reached up to him, pulled his head down, and kissed him hard on the lips. Her voice was low, tentative, almost a whisper.

'I'll see you in three months.'

He was silent, caught quite by surprise.

He listened to the sound of the car driving down the hill, thinking about how he and Olivia had taken it for granted that they would be married, some time soon, no need to specify a time, there was plenty of time. That was such a long time ago.

He dug his pass out of his pocket and waited for the guard to lift the barrier. The gate lifted, and he walked up the tarmac road. He recognised the smell of fuel carried on the wind. The nervous tension pooled in his stomach. As he walked, the anger he felt at Olivia's rejection dissolved and passed away.

The wind dropped and the parched grasses between the trees stood motionless. He stopped after a while to swap his bag to the other shoulder, wiping sweat from his forehead as he did so. It was the mid-day lunch period, and there was no-one around except for him. A transporter growled in the distance, far off on the perimeter of the launch-bed, then coughed to a halt as the operator killed the engine. He licked his dry lips, and, surprised again, tasted Harper's lipstick.

The base seemed like a well of silence. Going on along the road, the silence seemed to rise, and grow stronger, drowning the faint noise of the traffic on the autoroute away down the hill, drowning the song of the birds squabbling in the olive trees along the road. As he walked further into the base, he felt absorbed by the gigantic quiet; protected from the noise and the confusion of human affairs; freed from the blood and the mire of the world. He relaxed, flooded by peace. He would be flying soon.

Late that night Olivia looked at her watch and, with an air of reluctant release, uncrossed her legs on the sofa, making to go outside. Harper followed her up the hill.

They waited for longer than normal, and Harper took Olivia's hand after a time. At last, there appeared a burning light that rose and was lost among the stars.

They walked back down to the house in silence, both stumbling on the rough ground. Neither of them slept easily; the sky seemed darker and smoother than was normal for the time of the year, the stars burning more fiercely and the light more alien. If Olivia thought about it, to continue with the space program would have seemed wrong, not from the usual reason of cost, or lack of public interest, or even for the sake of John, but more from loneliness. She had seen the same library footage as John, at about the same age, but neither the power, the speed, nor the totality of the explosion affected her. What stunned her, leaving a horror that still lingered, was a vision of the people on board the shuttle, a fear of how it would be to die among such perfect blackness.

In her own room, Harper rested, trying to sleep, yet alive to a new excitement. She was thinking about how one simple kiss could realign everything.

4
INDIAN SUMMER

'There's a lock on the door, so don't worry; Old Fibroch won't get you tonight.'

The old man laughed to himself as he climbed the stairs. He had made the same joke every clear night for as long as the young man could remember. There were wild seas outside during the winter, but that night at least would be calm and starry, unworried, and warm. The young man followed him up to the light to watch the sun go.

'There aren't any moths on this island to beat against the light like they used to, back on the shore in the old days,' the old man said. He paused a while, looking out across the massive breadth of water, on to the narrow line of black on the horizon. 'There's no hiding it up here, you know.'

The sun swelled as it approached the horizon. The surface of the water became rough and pitted as the shadows produced by its own waves grew in the closing of a watery mesh.

'There are no lights on the coast over there and no ship has passed this way for ten years. I don't suppose there'll be any more now.' He was adrift now, and the young man lost in a dream of his own.

'It's a pity. I used to like the old ships with the dark red sails, going off to fight. Ah, but that was when we were capable of all that.'

He coughed once as the last sliver of the sun vanished beyond the curve of the sea; the summer had lasted longer than normal, but now it was ending and there was cold in the air.

'Now it would be good to see even a fishing boat.'

The two men walked down from the light, down the echoing stairwells and through worn out arches. They passed reeking cross passages, from which side breezes came to make the lantern flicker. At this, the old man guarded the flame against being engulfed by the warm, dripping dark. When he saw what the old man did, and how their shadows flickered, eerie on the rock walls, the young man smiled: he wasn't scared. On evenings when he looked after the flames alone—the summer nights when the old man walked outside, watching the lights play between the stars—he explored without a lantern. He found his way among the chambers and corridors lit by the veins of soft opalescent light which wound through the rock of the tower. Once, while following one of these lit paths, chasing a warm breeze, he came to a crumbled archway. The way ended in a mound of rubble alive with vines stretching to caress each other in the open air of the night, for beyond this arch was nothing. He sat there for hours on the edge of the tower. His legs dangled into the incredible drop, and he wondered for the first time at the builders of this lighthouse.

The woman walked into the blue glass room. The view was of vast plains of long, green grass, mountainous eruptions and divides, and dense forest land. After that, she could see breakers as the sea continued beyond her vision. This view of the entire world brought her calm, as it always did, and so the sound of the glass strung outside the window was pleasant. She walked through the blue glass room and out on to the balcony. Earlier she had seen the mauve and violet sky, which meant there was a storm far out to sea. Now the storm was fading, and the sun glowered as it touched the horizon. She watched as the shadows crept across country, leaping from hill to mountaintop as the sun squatted lower. Then they were at the base of her tower, far below. She waited until the top of the tower was the only thing still in light. Softer by tones, the incandescence faded, and the darkness returned.

This night clouds passed over the tower. Their lowest portions passed wraith-like around the blue glass room, dusting the millions of lines traced on the glass by the weather of a hundred years. When the moon shone, later, the greenish light within the room moved and flicker as the rustling web of whitened scratches shifted. As the woman slept, above her was the night. Around her were the shadows, and half a mile below her the ground laboured, heaving as earthshaping continued.

He saw the town as soon as he sailed past the crumbling chalk of the headland. Many houses and buildings lay half ruined; the slanting rays of the sun cast long, brown shadows which broke up the lines of the buildings. The village was old and long deserted; the damp wood lay rotting, swept up by the tide.

He landed and pushed the raft up the shingle of the beach. He got to the edge of the buildings, and now he could see that they were far older than he had thought. Few walls were standing; the rest had collapsed or were starting to. He looked further into the ruins and saw stone buildings that were still whole, their outsides painted a dull brown.

He found himself on a road, which was half-covered under a layer of dark green plants and weeds. He walked along the edge of the sea, around the bay of the town. He gazed along side streets, looking up often, for the town stood on hills that rose as they drew away from the sea. The streets wandered among rubble, then faltered and lost their shape, their outlines softening and defeated by the shards of wood, the broken buildings, and the stifling greenery. He saw signs men had lived there. Fragments of glassware, pottery, pieces of metal rusting on the edge of the sea, twisted and framing old purposes.

Then he found the boat. It was lying on its side on the beach, half-buried in drifting shale with shellfish ornamenting its exposed side. Its metal rigging was whole in places; elsewhere it broke free and described wild loops, curves dissolving into rust. He knew it to be the type of boat he had seen years before, wallowing and heaving in heavy seas away from land; or sailing past in fine summer weather, the sailors lounging at its rails. He saw why there had been no ships since he was a boy. After a time, he clambered on to the tilting deck and explored.

He found a locked room whose door gaped in a score of places; inside there were many chests. He pulled one open, and his strength was enough to lay out the yards of heavy sailcloth he found. But this coloured cloth no longer reminded him of blood. The colour had become softer. These were dusty red sails, tired desert sails. No longer, and perhaps never, man-of-war sails.

Before he left the boat, he draped the cloth over the hull and weighted it with stones from the beach. At the top of the next headland, he turned and looked back. The red ochre of the sails blended with the wooden ruins. He sat and looked at the scene until it became too dark to see the boat. The town seemed to creep nearer as night fell, absorbing light. He turned away and continued his walking, so he was not aware that when the moon rose the shadows reappeared on the ruins and the red sail returned to prominence.

She once spent days by a pool in one room in the tower: bathing, swimming, and diving, then drying on the bank under trees. In this room there were birds, and she watched them soar high above her in a continuous wheeling motion. They made designs against the blue of the roof, patterns that became as intricate as the scratches on the glass of her bedroom, yet living and defying memory and knowledge.

When she slept there, she dreamed of ancient war and the heat of the sun.

He paused for breath halfway up the last slab of dark rock. There was a ledge there, with an abandoned nest tucked into the corner. Earlier, he had frightened an entire colony of birds. He could still hear the squawking as they spilled over the edge and dropped into space at his approach. He turned and pressed against the rock and slid into a sitting position. From this position high among the range of mountains, he could trace his path of the last months. He could see where he began, and the marshes around the river-mouth that had forced him away from the seashore. His eyes glazed after a while, and he stayed motionless until the sun moved behind the rock he was climbing. Vision returned, and he shivered. The old man had died; something had gone wrong with his insides and had eaten him away. Yet he did not feel as though half of himself had died, as he had supposed he would in the time the old man was worst; instead, he felt calm, whole. Once or twice, wonderful whenever it happened, there had been schools of dolphins around the lighthouse. He had watched them twist from the water and willed them not to re-enter that region where they were invisible to him. In the exercise of such complete concentration, he had found a solitude and a peace such that he had not minded when the dolphins overcame him and disappeared back beyond his perception.

When he found the body of a baby dolphin washed up on the rocks, he had felt as if he had triumphed. Even so, the fact of the young death bothered him until the body began to smell. He realised all this had nothing to do with him.

It was late by the time he reached the summit, and the sun had nearly disappeared. He had not expected the massive plains of dark grass that stretched out on the other side; he had thought that the world was smaller. But it was not this that caused a flashing, shuddering, shock-filled blindness, and it was not this that caused him to stagger and double over, feeling a knot of implication in his stomach. In the middle of this plain, grim in its simple, familiar newness, was a massive tower whose glass top glinted an alien blue through the dusk gathering around it.

She ran down the corridor, down stairs, through dusty galleries, past the doors of darkness, the rooms of masks and mirrors, and the pit that sometimes held stars. She came to a room of gardens, hanging flowers, fountains, and she became calmer; but she knew something had changed; the smoke she had seen climbing from the nearest mountain that morning told her as much. She was no longer alone, and she greeted the stark division of the sky with warmth.

He had made the fire for reasons beyond his reach. Despite the sudden knowledge that he was a minute figure between the sky and the land, and the other knowledge that he loomed giant and unhideable amongst the barren rocks, he had made the fire from new green growth. The smoke had poured and smothered skyward in a choking pall, and, as he looked behind him now, he could still see a lean streak of grey staining the midday blue. He was becoming unwell; he had a headache and, for the first time since he had left the lighthouse, he was tired in a way that made him feel old. In daylight, the top of the tower lost its brilliant light, but the tower itself gained strength and solidity until it became as natural an outcropping as any mountain. It was there in his sleep, night after night. It sat in landscapes that distorted and grew feverish, yet it remained rigid and compulsive, dominating his sleep until he yelled and woke to see the stars covered in haze.

She had tied the fragments of glass outside the window many years before. Sometimes when she lay in bed, she imagined that their jangling became cries of pain in the piercing wind. Half-asleep as she was, this disturbed her, and she grabbed the bedclothes more tightly around her until the warmth made her mind peaceful again and she could dream more easily.

The weather changed. Noise from storms over the mountains he had crossed reached him through the day, reminding him of the sea and the old man. He walked across the plain, the ground undulating, and the grass tall enough to prevent a clear view of the entire horizon. The feathery ears and leaves of grass welled up, catching the wind, and isolating him from the horizon he moved towards. He walked in cells of green roofed by grey. At these moments, when the horizon no longer formed a massive frame, he was in a floating bubble. It was like the times he closed his eyes under water and let himself be carried by the warm currents flowing around the light-house island. Then the wind would flatten the grass again and he could see along the channels impressed on the bowed grass towards the tower.

She watched him advance across the surface of the plain, his progress discernible at first only from the fires he made each sundown; then leaping into view one morning as a moving dot on the furthest stretches of her vision. She stayed for the first few days in the blue glass room at the very top of the tower, but then made her way down the various levels. She paused for hours in rooms looking out the relevant way. She tried to make out any movement which could reflect the intent of the creature that, each night, lit a fire closer along the straight line which led to the base of her tower. When she first perceived the moving dot, she froze; then, when she recognised him as being like herself, she moved down through the remaining few levels of the tower to the door that she had never used.

One morning, he was very close. She found the door opened easily enough in the end, and she moved outside the tower to meet him.

He watched as the sky grew more overcast. He welcomed the pain in his head brought by the pressure of the approaching storm; with it came the prospect of resolution. For days, he had felt eyes upon him; he felt eyes with perceptions and emotions different from anything he had experienced. Fear and revulsion mixed in his mind with the obsessive drive onward, and he felt himself carried along in a way that ignored what he thought he needed. He arrived at the base of the tower and squatted, muscles tense and locked, waiting for release. It came. The door opened and a naked figure like, but not like his own, came out and towards him. It approached and paused in front of him. He looked, at first with a blank mind, then with increasing comprehension and hatred. A wall was being built as he watched; a wall built of the million desires and fears and conversations and directions that appeared as he waited. The future had meaning—and it engulfed him.

The grey sky cracked, and the clouds of grey plate steel pressed on the earth. Adam, more scared than he had ever been in his life, drawing awful energy from the pelting, hissing rain, moved with stiff-legged intent towards the woman.

5
OLD, PERSISTENT SPIRITS

Barbaric green; cool and dark. Slime coated muscle, flexing, unflexing; rhythm pushing through the clouded, pea-green sea, driving through the mackerel and the herring, the snapper and the krill. I know it; I feel it near—the black eyes, dull as smoke, the silver scales, the massive fin high over the water—tall, spiny, swaying with each wave breached, moving in a slow, patterned trembling that reflects the control, the strength, and the anger of the fish.

What of me, as I flounder among white crested sheets, soaked by foaming nightmare, drenched by the unknown? It's my ship, my men, that the fish diverts into panic. Young lads converted to soothsaying like the oldest, believing in the throw of dice, the turn of a wave or the pattern of cast grain.

Thoughts of solid, compactible earth comfort all, memories of secure sleep amongst mountains bring a ship-wide desire for forest, hill, valley, and city—anything for an escape from the community of the waves, the scorching of the oceanic winds, and the fear of the great fish that haunts our passage.

It began with ice, exploration, and greed, and will end with the sea around us. This I know, this we all know. Feet pound the deck above my head and the moment for resolution approaches, but I delay in my cot.

Among the icy mountains on an island off the southmost tip of the southmost lands, there, where our dogs limped in the cold, on a ledge on a mountainside, by a cave mouth, Mr Maglip started us on this tragedy. The carvings on the lintel were obscene. I should have shot him and had him cut up for the dogs. But the dogs were tied up away down the mountain, the crew needed paying, and my judgement was weaker than my greed.

I looked away from the ancient obscenities above the cave mouth, warning off intruders, ordered Stover and Crane to light their torches, and we started. The way was simple, a short, right-angled passage leading to a small room, a mere hollow among the rocks, no real protection. Maglip's box was there as he had forecast, as old and heavy as he had foretold; yet the handles were strong and our ropes held, and we hauled this crate down a thousand feet of eroded track, slipping and cursing, the snow under our feet turning our ankles. Maglip was animated beyond excitement, working alongside the cabin boy, sharing the strain, his old joints popping and his white hair damp with sweat. We all sweated, dangerous in that cold air, and we worked the faster to stop the sweat freezing into cracking plates in our armpits and on our scalps.

We were fools. It may have been that the influence of the thing in the box was already working, uniting us, pulling us together, making us heedless of the wind and the snow—or perhaps Maglip's reckless energy was enough to fire us and bring us to stupid life. We were fools though, because, out of all the hands there, all the wise sailors and nervous boys, there was no-one that remarked on the fact that the box was coffin sized, coffin shaped, with brass handles and shiny nails along its fine wooden top.

Oh, there's no body in there, there's no need for these dreams I keep having, these illusions of a miraculously preserved woman. No, there are no ghosts on this ship— and no saints either, glowing in the dark with their holy peace and their quiet bones. But the shape of the box was no coincidence because I know what's in there. I and a couple of the men took the top off early yesterday morning, and I've met the demon that brought sad old Mr Maglip all this way.

I can hear the shouting in the gangways. Soon I will have to act. I turn under my blanket and rehearse the parts of this catastrophe once more. How we got the cargo on board. How the ship slipped back through the ice-covered rocks and turned her nose back to the north. How the sucking and the rolling of the wintry sea couldn't bother us as we rode out the blow. We were happy in this charter of a lifetime and that strange Mr Maglip was going to make us all rich.

For night after night, the light of the hanging lanterns bucked with the twists of the ship. The men crammed in on kegs and canvas chairs to drink and sing. Maglip sat with us, soaking it up, sitting at the centre of it all, taking up a seat with his back to the base of the mizzen mast. His hands would be folded in his lap, and he would drink little, but he would beam around him and incline his head, murmuring filthy stories in the most dignified tones. Everyone had a mug of brandy and—I remember, it is true—there was genuine relief that the worst was over.

We reached Patagonia and followed the coast north with gathering speed, day by day leaving the cold regions and reaching warmer air. We paused for a moment as the land finished. Then, elated by our fortune, we unfurled more canvas to take an extra gulp of breeze, leaving the mainland and setting out over the Gulf.

So, it was good, until one morning two days ago. The rising sun rose hot, flattening the waves, and the water was green to a depth of darkness beyond our sight. Becalmed we hove to, far away from land. One by one, the men came on deck and gathered at the rails, looking into the water. Fresh conversation blossomed; new jokes were told. Then all the men fell silent with awe: below the ship there passed flash after flash of silver. A torrent of mercury paused around us, grew more intense, filling the water around the ship with light. The summer of the trip had arrived, and the men grew agitated, wanting to be among the shoal of mackerel, bathing with the fish, washing off their winter dirt.

I gave the permission and ordered Crane and Croker to row with the rifle and a pistol to one hundred yards. Maglip humoured our mood, saying 'Aye aye, Cap'n', winking at me and clambering with my gun onto the roof of the wheelhouse. He rode there, straddling the rolling ship, showing a happy, long-toothed smile.

The younger men jostled by the rail on the lowest part of the deck, stripping their clothes off, laughing with the sudden arrival of summer. I checked the water, and smelled the breeze, and gave a glance to the sky. All was good. I looked down to smile at the lads before giving the order:

'Hands to bathe!'

They jumped, pushed, and slipped into the water, all white skin and thin limbs. I watched them splash for a while, then leaned over the rail and looked for mermaids as if I were young and stupid. In the morning's calm and the warmth of the rising sun, my thoughts drifted. I wondered about the box we had covered the ocean to retrieve, and I wondered about Maglip once more. I had passed by his stateroom door that morning and once again seen the portrait he had hung on his cabin wall. The woman was young, and beautiful, but the clothes were old-fashioned, and the frame was not new. As the voyage had progressed, I grew to suspect that Maglip and I had something in common. Thoughts about my Eleanor, my wife began again.

It's easy to imagine the woman you love; the way you know her, and talk to her, and how she is with you; but it's not so straightforward to find her. It's easy to rake around in all the flesh of the world, but when you find the one, hold on with your teeth gritted and your feet dug in. If you let her slide past you through laziness, or ignorance, the odds are you'll never get another chance.

I was lucky—I had warning. One night when I was young, I dreamed of this woman, and in the dream there was no question; she was the only woman there could ever be. Then, one year, two years later, I met her, and with that powerful dream behind me, I had no choice. I loved her without thinking, without remission.

The other thing about the perfect woman is that she will never, ever leave you. It isn't possible, it could never enter her head, because you are a part of her as well. Yet sometimes these perfect women do go; sometimes they die.

Then the blast of a gun kicked a waterspout out of the sea.

The task of the men in the boat, and Maglip above my head, was to forget about how much they wanted to be baptised again in that beautiful ocean. They had to watch the water and to keep the rifle ready. It was their job to see the first fin to break the surface near my lads. They had to shout and bellow and wash those sailors back into the ship on the wave of their noise, and then they had to blast away at that fin and scare off the shark.

I saw the pair in the boat a long way out, Crane standing, shouting, waving his arms, and Croker facing out to sea, trying to steady the rifle, leaning forwards, back bent to keep his balance like a man with a burden at the end of outstretched arms. As I watched them, their boat rose on the hump of a giant wave, as something massive passed close beneath it. They lost their balance and tumbled over; Crane to the floor in the bows and Croker hanging out over the stern.

Another shot exploded close by, and Maglip shouted a curse. I turned to look up. His face was white, contorted, and he was clumsy as he brandished the gun, how he pointed the barrel randomly, far beyond his intention.

I crouched, stunned and helpless against such chaos. I looked through the rail at what was happening in the water. The crew swarmed towards the ship. Furious paddle, breaststroke, dog stroke; those that were strong swimmers leaving the others to flounder. And behind them, giant and purposeful through the glassy sea, was a single fin. Yet, the three men with guns were as dangerous as the fish. Crane, Croker and Maglip were shooting at the shark, but they were panicked, and between them were peppering the whole of the water between the ship and the fish. I could do nothing for the men on the boat, but Maglip was within reach.

As the first of the boys in the water reached the bottom of the ladder, I hauled myself up the steps to the wheelhouse. I stopped, shocked at Maglip's terror. His lips fixed wide open over clenched teeth. He was crying. His shoulders shook as he pulled the barrel of the gun around in sweeping arcs, trying to fix his aim, loosing off shot after shot.

I shouted his name, and I lurched towards him, but he made no sign of hearing. At the last possible moment, he caught a hint of me coming. He began a low groan from his throat that lasted as we toppled across the wheelhouse roof and then over the edge.

We landed hard and lay tangled whilst the ship wallowed and I panted, winded. I got up first, and I limped round to the other side of the ship. I willed myself on despite the prospect of the slaughter the shark and Crane and Croker had combined to inflict. I steadied myself against the ladder to the quarter-deck and focused, looking for the massacre I expected. All I could see were sailors sitting wetly on the deck, their legs through the rails, faces lit by the sun, shouting happy abuse at the two men in the boat as they moored to the bottom of the ladder. Of the shark, there was no sign.

That was the beginning of the fish. Dazed after my fall, I took to my bunk. Even though there were no injuries, I knew I had lost my grip. I was already dreaming of the shining thing in the box down in the hold; its influence was already winding around the timbers of the ship. I didn't know this, so I didn't understand why suddenly I was obsessed by too many memories.

Then a twin disaster stormed into my cabin. Maglip came first, furious, unsteady on his feet, as dazed and sickened by the fall as me. He raged at me; there had been a theft from his box. Something small and valuable was missing. All the merchant navy were scum, and we had forfeited our charter. Then came Breecher. He was weary and upset, talking about a body overboard, a man lost at sea. God alone knew how, in the glass sea we coasted over, but Mejzner had vanished. He had not been swimming with the rest.

I issued commands, they slackened the sheets, and the

ship wheeled and turned. I posted men to watch, and we lowered the boat in preparation. We sailed backwards and forwards, trawling for the boy. We turned about and about for hours, sweeping the length of the waves in ever widening, ever more hopeless circles. The afternoon came, and went, but nowhere was there sign of a swimmer. Maglip paced around, silent and angry until, all but ignored, he disappeared back under deck. We covered and recovered the same area of sea until all hope was gone.

It was Maglip himself who resolved both our problems with his triumphant shout.

'I've got your boy!'

He stood behind us all, in the middle of the ship.

'And I've found my thief.'

There, slung between his arms like a hammock, was Mejzner's naked body. Behind him, his face clamped, was Breecher. A murmur came up from the men. Maglip spoke to them.

'May I commend Mr Breecher to you! He was the only one of you all with any brains!'

The taut silence proved how Maglip had misjudged this announcement, but Breecher spoke up for him.

'It's true. Mejzner was the man who broke into this gentleman's freight. He slashed himself, lying in a corner behind a bulwark right on top of the dirty ballast.'

While I tried to fathom what was not being told, and the men murmured and groaned, Maglip forgot his place, and shouted an order to the men.

'There's no more to it—the boy killed himself. He was lovesick, like a child.'

Suddenly, Maglip's voice had too much of an aristocratic whine for the men. Mejzner had been liked, and suicide was unbelievable. There were shouts and men clustered around the two of them. Their anger was growing too fast. I stepped forward.

'All hands—to their posts. Mr Breecher—help Mr Maglip to his room. Crane, Croker—half a mug of rum for every man while we dress Mr Mejzner.'

The body was prepared there and then, for we were far into the tropics. We said prayers, we had some singing, and I officiated as the boy, dressed in a canvas sack, slid away from us over the side of the ship.

Without warning, the fin slid from the water only twenty feet from the side of the ship. While we watched, the fish took Mejzner. None of us could have been prepared for that—there was little blood in the water; the sand of the ballast had soaked most of that up; but the shark took him hard and fast, and everyone who was looking saw the torn flesh.

Maglip laughed, loud in the silence. The men gazed at him, shocked into inaction. He put a hand over his mouth to stifle the laughter, casting an eye over the faces of the crew, but continuing, his shoulders heaving. Breecher walked in front of him. With his face upturned and six inches away from Maglip's, he murmured,

'Didn't you see what happened, sir? The shark had Mejzner.'

'Oh dear!' Maglip carried on, wheezing as his cheeks reddened and his hair fell forwards. Breecher looked patient.

'I don't see the humour, sir.'

Maglip stopped. He wiped his mouth with his hand as he looked at Breecher.

'I had thought that you owned a rudimentary wit, Mr Breecher, but I'm not so sure now. I don't need to point out to an old sailor like you how that fish isn't the remotest family to a shark.'

Breecher stared at him.

'I don't care what it is sir, I don't see the humour.'

Maglip stopped smiling. I saw something deep, something like fear, behind his unblinking eyes.

'I never expected you to. And stay away from my box.'

My recognition came too late. Maglip lashed out and knocked a surprised Breecher backwards. As a man, the crew descended on Maglip; with that laughter, he had annihilated their respect for him. I let the fight go on far too long, and I was glad when Maglip begged me for protection. I locked him up in his cabin as much to let the crew get on with their mourning as for his safety.

I returned to lie in my cot and drink brandy and brood on how things would resolve themselves now I had arrested the patron of the entire enterprise. The airless evening faded, and night came down over the ship, and then another, more terrifying presence invaded my thoughts.

Around midnight I snuffed out my candle the better to listen to the silence that had fallen over the ship. There was no sound except my breathing and the creaking of the joints in my neck as I turned my head from side to side, trying to catch the atmosphere. Pictures came to me, carried on a jolt of tension that burned around the edges of my door. I listened to the hiatus over the ship, as if each man had stopped talking and was suspended, straining to catch knowledge of what was approaching.

There was the slightest grating sound, as if the ship had brushed the most delicate acquaintance with a bank of shale. I held my breath. This could not be. We were in the middle of the Gulf.

Then there was the first collision. In normal times, the waist of the ship would have been flooded with men struggling past each other to get out on deck. But each man on board knew we were three hundred miles from the nearest shore, floating, pressed against the gulping black of the sea by the smothering night. There was no tropical island jostling our shoulder with its calypso and its greenery; we were all too mindful of the precarious height of the ship above the dark seabed.

The next collision was louder. I could hear the individual sounds of each man on board leaning backwards, slipping lower into his bunk. What fish would attack a ship in this way? The blows came quicker, vibrating through the ship. We have a good oak keel, sheathed in copper, and it transmitted each booming impact. Again, a collision, and this time the ship seemed to shift in the water. Then silence. Then a grazing, tantalising blow. And another.

Sometimes it felt as if the fish swam directly into the ship, jarring even to the upper decks in a head on attack; sometimes the ship trembled with a brushed touch. I lay in bed, sweating in the hot air of the night, waiting in agony for each echoing collision, and wondering, like the rest of them, what it was we carried that could attract such awful attention.

Towards dawn, the blows stopped, and I slipped towards sleep. But I hear things lying in my bunk, and the night had put an edge on all my senses. The ship is formed from resonant timber, and sounds will trickle in at an opened porthole. Towards dawn, voices came to me. I overheard Breecher talking, soft, urgent, to the other low voices of the watch.

'And I tell you, was there, wrists opened...'

I pondered on how I had lost the boy Mejzner to death. That was no small thing. It is true he had been unhappy. His girl didn't love him, and he took joy from this. In return for her disdain, he loved her as much as any man could love a woman, and she hurt him on the same colossal scale. But he was young, and unconfident, and had steered clear of the polished Maglip. So how had Maglip known the reason for his suicide?

Breecher's words drifted down as I wondered; inflammatory, excited, inciting.

'... the fish? You reckon on bad spirits, don't you? A bad spirit come to get back that casket. Maybe ... but I've seen what Maglip's after. I've seen what this whole trip's been for. The boy had stolen alright; you believe it, because I saw what he had in his hand. I think we got a whole trunk of it in the hold ... The boy had got three knuckle bones wrapped tight in his fingers, and Maglip snatched them back. They shone like gold. We should look in the hold sometime while the captain's laid up and Maglip's out of the way. Let's get us some real good luck.'

Wisps of cirrus; white clouds in the violet evening sky. I am old and weather-wise, and I recognise the approaching tempest.

So, I peered into the box in the hold this last morning. The men were terrified of the fish, and I foresaw mutiny. But Croker has never been a coward and Crane was always willing to take a chance on a new adventure. Perhaps, like me, they scented greatness above gold, something unbelievable in the hold of our ship.

It was oppressive, dark, and hot, and we sweated. We followed in Mejzner's footsteps and pried up the lid of the ancient box. The nails yielded, the lid swung back, and a skeleton grinned back at us. It was a small skeleton, like the skeleton of a child, but it gleamed in the candlelight. It was a skeleton of solid gold, with each joint a large ball of ruby fitting into a polished ivory cup. The box was lined and padded with a dark velvet, and the bones, the skeleton, lay there, somehow poised, taut, and supple, the knees bent, the thighs raised a fraction, and the arms in a natural position, as if held in place by an invisible musculature. The rib cage and the hips curved, swelling out almost unnaturally to suggest the shape of the body they would support. And the head, the skull; ivory teeth inset into the golden jaws, forming a whitened grin, a gold and old ivory smile. The head lay, tilted back, darkened sockets somehow holding memories of eyes.

We were silent for a moment in marvelling at the thing —and as we watched, I noticed an essence, a presence, settling into the struts of gold, draping itself across the framework in a ghostly flesh. This was not the skeleton of a child, but of a woman. Eleanor, all the images of years ago, came into my mind with the crackle of electricity. At that moment all I could think, was that she was around me, that she was near.

Flesh coalescing on the bones? Perhaps. Or yearning, loneliness, and the power of the skeleton. But I saw then what I couldn't bear to watch for long. Flesh settled on to the bones, drew together over the bones; that soft, dark skin, the face, the breasts, that same rich, almost heavy body. I had wanted this return for so long.

There we stood, whitened faces standing out in the dark of the hold like gawkers at a carnival side show. Like three thirsty men stumbling upon a gushing stream of cold, clear water, we stood and drank it in. Crane looked to be on the verge of tears. Stoker gazed, hopeful, his beaten-up face restored to youth. I couldn't stand it. I wrenched the lid up with both hands and slammed it against the box to break the spell.

'Eva!' shouted Stoker. 'Eva!'

Equally devastated, Crane shouted a name, too. The woman he had seen in the box was called Diana.

I grabbed them by their shirts and dragged the two of them out. I came back with a hammer and a fistful of long nails and pounded the box lid until the wood bruised around each nail head. I nailed the box shut, and then I nailed closed the door to the hold.

Maglip, I knew what he was doing—and who in their right minds could blame him? He had found a way to abandon himself—or restore himself; and he had ignored the catastrophe following on behind. But then no-one could have left a thing like that once heard of.

Perhaps one of his ancestors made the skeleton, saw what he had done, and buried it for us to find—or perhaps it was much, much older than that. Perhaps it was carried there on a papyrus raft, a raft that sailed seas of thickening ice, the crew lost, but unable to bear losing their cargo. Of course, every man on board this ship would sell his soul to possess it; Mejzner was only the first to take the risk.

A day passed. An airless day spent becalmed under the sun, the men gathered into groups in the shade, muttering, telling each other's fortunes, Maglip shouting and banging in his cabin. When night came, the fish returned, rasping and banging against the hull until the ship reeked of sweat and fear. Only at dawn did it leave us, and even then I slept but poorly. Memories of Eleanor, impressions of attainable bliss tormented me. The past was returning, and my excitement was driving me half insane. But as I dozed, I fancied I could hear noises beneath me, in the hold.

I awoke to a sound I expected for two days: angry shouting, running feet, something large and heavy being dragged up the stairs. I picked up my rifle and moved out of my cabin off into the waist of the ship.

I paused at the top of the companion ladder. The men had got to the box and carried it out onto the deck. They attacked the ancient wood with crowbars and spikes, crowding round one another, shouting, and even as I emerged, they ripped it open. I stepped closer. The skeleton was undiminished, lambent, beautiful. The men were bashful at first, then they recovered. The delicate fantasies created in the intimate dark of the hold tore and blew apart on the lust and longing, and the fight began again. Breecher had hold of the shoulders, and Carver and Stoker had hold of a leg each, and between them they were pulling the thing apart.

A drawn-out cry of pain rang out across the deck, coming from behind me. Like pure energy, Maglip burst past me, head low and shoulders braced. He loosed two rounds from two pistols, and part of the crowd swayed downwards. He growled and screamed, and threw himself among them, relying on the force of his surprise to claw his way through. His rage was enough, and he passed out of the front of the crowd as cleanly as he had charged into them; but on his way, he had gained hold of the skeleton. He ran as far forward as he could, staggering under the weight, then turned and faced them, clutching the golden skeleton across his chest with one arm, waving a pistol with the other. The men stood, astounded.

Then, as he rested against the rails, his chest heaving for breath, there came a heart-stopping collision at the bows. Then another, and another. He panted and leaned backwards out over the rail, looking sideways down at the water. He laboured up onto the bowsprit and steadied himself there among the forestays, shouting to us.

'Even the fish knows its value! Why do you want to destroy it? Are you all as stupid as you act?'

The fish was pounding the timbers down below him, driven momentarily crazy. He leaned backwards and took aim downwards. He fired and cursed.

A cool wind was blowing, and he turned his face into it, closing his eyes for a moment. Panting still, he flicked his tongue around his lips and fumbled another round into the gun. He aimed downwards again, taking his time, then he fired. We watched, helpless. He looked up and smiled. There was colossal relief on his face.

'I've hit it. It's flesh after all!'

He pointed and laughed.

'Look, it's bleeding!'

There was a leaden pause, all the men waiting for me, arms by their side, sullen, unhappy. I could so easily lose them.

Maglip tried again. 'Look, it's finished.' He laughed. He waved his arm, expansive. 'Come and watch the fish flee. We can go home. You'll get paid now.'

His influence was waning. Crane looked at the body at his feet and took a step forwards, the men behind him.

Maglip and his treasure had proved to me that Eleanor still existed somewhere, and as long as I knew of the skeleton, I would fight anyone for the having of it. I looked at the men, how they mustered nerve, how poised they were. Here was a disaster.

I raised the rifle and shouted something. Maglip looked up at me. He wasn't afraid, but furious. His stare fixed on me, ignoring for a moment the men closing on him. Crane was at the front of the crowd. I shouted his name, ordered him to stop. Maglip jeered at me:

'How you discipline your crew!'

He raised his pistol and pointed it at Crane's stomach.

'Don't come any closer.'

There was a pause and then Breecher and Croker shouldered their way through the crowd to stand at Crane's shoulders. I sighted Maglip down the rifle. He decided; he lifted his arm and swung the barrel to cover all three of them. He made his choice and fired a shot. Breecher fell and the other two rushed for Maglip.

It was easy. With all the time I needed, I squeezed the trigger. The force of the shot knocked him backwards. He tangled amongst the forestays. I squinted down the barrel at him and fired again. He jolted backwards and released the skeleton, toppling into the sea. The skeleton balanced for a moment, caught in the mess of lines, and followed him into the water.

Every man on board dived to the rail, and we strained our eyes to see into the green depths of the water, to witness the conclusion. There it was: a great black shape rushed in from afar, there was a flash of gold, a retreat, and then we were left.

I am the captain on board, and it is the captain's job to shepherd his crew. The men under my command had discovered the skeleton, and the knowledge could produce only greed and lust. I hated myself for letting the secret out. I hated myself for allowing too many people to see what I could have kept to myself. But more, much, much more:

You have haunted me, Eleanor, for years too long.

Maglip had a way for me to slip further backward into the shadow of her spirit. I'd been with her for every day of these last fifteen years; now I was tired, I wanted to rest; I wanted her to leave me.

So, the resolution came easy. Things started with greed, and they ended in violence and the sea. Great men are devious and rise to evil as it meets their needs. I have never been great, but it took me only a moment to slip the key to Maglip's cabin under his door, and less time than that to drop the brace of pistols on the stairwell where he had no choice but to stumble over them.

Once buried, love should never be exhumed.

6

IN THE DAYS OF INCREASING AUTOMATION

The house rested in the late evening. The distant church bell sounded, the notes rolling down along the coast. Only a few hundred feet in front of the house, across the road, there was the sea.

The roof of the house lay on wooden rafters. These in their turn rested on wooden beams and dark wooden walls, all cut from the forest whose fragments gathered around the house this evening.

The sun had been hot in the afternoon, and the house was moving now, shifting in shadowed corners. Creaking boards touched, complaining as they shed the warmth of the day. The roof relaxed on the dry walls; the floorboards yawned into bigger gaps and settled more heavily on the joists. There was little moisture even in the darkest corners of the cellar, where the blind and reeking earth and brick mouldered into each other. Tiny cracks appeared, larger cracks stretched out to each other, hastening their eventual meeting.

The noise of a distant car broke the silence. It was a very long way away, but it grew louder. The door to the house opened. A woman stepped out onto the veranda. She held the door open behind her for a moment, whilst she listened, head on one side. She nodded to herself. Shutting the door behind her, stepped forward to hold on to the balcony. As she waited, a great smile forced itself onto her face.

The car roared up the drive and skidded into the sand piled up next to the house. Ben and Leon threw open the doors and raced up the dark earth path to the porch veranda. They shouted their greetings up to her. She stood in the lamplight, leaning back against a pillar, arms folded, beaming at them.

They vaulted the balustrade, one after the other. Their blond hair and their smooth, suntanned skin and the muscles in their backs carried them up and over. They landed lightly, recovered easily, Ben bowing and laughing. He gathered her up to embrace her and kissed her.

'Lisa, you wouldn't believe it this time—Ali and Kirsty have had twins—'

'—they're so beautiful—'

'—they've bought land out there on the river bend, you know, back up by the old chapel.'

'They want everyone they know to get out there and live there and work the place with them, they've got no idea...'

'But we said no way, and then we said, maybe, and then we thought about the summer in the islands, and we could all go over there, and...'

The clamour tumbled into the house. Leon stopped, suddenly humble: 'Have you still got a room here for me, Mrs Clinton?'

Lisa swiped at him, and he disappeared up the stairs with his backpack, leaving Ben and Lisa to go into the kitchen.

Ben struck a match and went around all the oil lamps, dropping the match as it burnt his fingers, talking all the while. He turned the main lights off, turned to Lisa for approval—and realised his selfishness.

'Ah, I didn't ... How are you?'

'I'm getting along fine,' Lisa said.

'I'm sorry. You should've stopped me. When Leon's around, I get carried away.'

'Ben, you know that's OK.'

She grinned and opened her arms. They embraced until she pulled away. She looked at him. 'You've been away a long time. Did you miss me?'

He nodded quickly and kissed her. She sighed and relaxed on him, laying her head on his shoulder. They stood together for a minute until there was a crashing from outside. The kitchen door burst open, and Leon fell into the room, red-faced and panting, holding a huge red ice chest with two hands. As he came in, he pushed a case of beers along with his foot. He gave a last effort, and the case slid to a standstill next to the table.

'Ok, you two, remember to breathe. Hey Lisa, did you know your old man's a big game hunter?'

Ben leaped up, took the chest from Leon, and hooked a chair out of the way with his foot. He put the chest down on the old wooden table. He opened it, and hauled out the great fish that was inside, holding it up with both hands, swivelling so Lisa could see.

'You are joking? You seriously think you can gut that all over my kitchen?'

'She's right, Leon,' said Ben. 'You know how it is with fish scales; they get everywhere. It doesn't matter it took a day and a half to land, then it killed two of the guys on the boat as it kicked around until I thrashed it with my bare hands and killed it with my teeth—if it makes any sort of mess in here then—I—Lisa!'

He ducked and twisted, face creasing with laughter as Lisa picked up a broom. She chased him around the table, his hands up, pleading with her. She laughed and swung the broom. Too hard. She lost her grip, and it connected square in Ben's chest, and he back-pedalled. He flailed his arms for comic effect, but then he tripped backwards over the case of beer and sat down hard.

'See how the mighty fall,' she crowed. She nudged him with the handle. 'You're getting old.'

Ben stood up, grinning, rubbing his back. Then his expression changed.

'Ben! What is it, Ben?'

His face blanked, and he staggered. He moved his mouth and his throat worked, but there was no sound.

'Ben! What's wrong?'

He stumbled and fell, dropping, landing hard.

'Ben!'

Leon bent and helped Ben up, grunting with the effort. 'It's alright Lisa. Could you go upstairs and turn down the bed? Ben needs a rest.'

'But ...'

'It's OK. Look out, here we go!'

Despite her protestations, Leon got Ben upstairs, put him to bed, and cooed over him like a baby. Lisa watched this, until she realised she was being excluded, when she left them to it.

Back in the kitchen, she pulled a beer out of the crate, opened it, and sat down at the kitchen table. She took a gulp and smiled. She knew when the day had turned bad; it had been on the way home from town.

She had given up early today. The heat had beaten her. Here, at the salted, sweating edge of England, the heat was a genuine issue for people like her; nowadays the climate was no fun, no fun at all. She had caught the bus back along the sea road. The bus was old, but still gleaming, a great chrome and sunburst parody of the old-style vehicles she still just about remembered. The bus pulled off, coping with the pitted road; they'd stopped repairing the potholes years ago. She'd sat and watched the woman across from her. She was old and looked like she had been there for days. It was possible; the driverless buses cruised day and night, following the same path, stopping for passengers, avoiding other traffic, following the Highway Code.

Ben had once explained how they, and, she presumed, he himself, navigated, but the details escaped her now.

The woman had taken out a square of silk. She laid it across her knees, and folded it into thirds lengthwise, then folded it again into a neat package. She twitched at the hem of her skirt, laying it straight along her legs, and brushed away invisible dust. She muttered to herself as she took one corner of the square and shook the folded package out. She laid the square across her knees and began folding it again.

'…so, he gave me pearls and everything, but he wasn't that old, and when he was up and leaving, he says; "Now you be sure to call me in writing, do you hear?"'

Lisa had looked at the woman's white hair, wisps glued to a taut skull, and listened.

'Every morning I'd wait for him to show his cheap face; every morning he'd turn up, regular as clockwork …'

There couldn't be a bigger tearjerker than this. Age, the real sob story. Didn't affect the bus, though. It had been running this route for as long as she could remember. Bits dropped off, sure; wheels punctured, chrome rusted. Occasionally, the engine would spark and seize up, but that wasn't the point; the brain of the thing carried on. Like most artificials, the bus was a total moron, but it got around. It loved to drive; it had a flair for dodging traffic; it adored scanning chip implants, and, in its own fresh-faced way, it was especially courteous to frail old ladies. Like Lisa.

Lord knows, she'd been young once, even been a toddler, round-faced, wondering. She'd had fat arms and legs browned by the sun; every day there was early breakfast with her mother, and then she played in the garden, no taller than the grass and certainly greener, chatting to field-mice and blackbirds, as unformed as the day. She knew all this. It had all happened to her once, but it all seemed so far away. She and Ben had been a young couple once; had jumped on a bus and left the city when it seemed inevitable. They could do that then; anything had been possible to her—even keeping up with Ben.

She thought of that trip down from Newcastle, over half a lifetime away. She had a memory, stashed away like a nugget of gold. They were lying on a grassy bank somewhere in the middle of Somerset while the coach driver refuelled. They were both dazed by the travel and the heat, and Lisa had put her head on Ben's chest and gazed at a statue in the middle of the town square. The statue had been beautiful; weathered yet unblemished. Over the years, lichen had enhanced the skill of the sculptor. It had added fine, organic detail: green feathers to the wings, moss to the hair, green velvet to the gown. The face was upturned, tilting back towards heaven, supplicating, the sinews of the neck standing out in exquisite relief. The uplifted hands were delicate; still, pure chiselled stone, long, fine fingers.

Lisa remembered how they had waited there in silence for what could have been an age. Every moment the sheer fact of the stone angel had passed more to her, shared more with her, poured strength and courage upon her. She still, after all these years, knew how she had felt, soaking in that experience of perfection.

She finished the last of the beer, yawned, and stood up. Of course, that was the pull. It was only nowadays that she understood why. She had thought that in some mystical way, if she stayed around Ben long enough, if she did as he did, went everywhere with him, then what he had, the strength of being made, not born, would somehow rub off on her. But of course, it hadn't. And look at tonight. Now she was old, and it was much too late.

She waited. Half an hour passed. She heard talking upstairs, then sudden laughter. Light flooded into the stair-well as the bedroom door opened. Leon came downstairs and into the kitchen. He was smiling to himself. She got up, motioned towards the other chair at the table, and gave him a beer and the opener. She sat down again in silence, then nodded her head, getting up to fetch him a glass.

'Ok. What's happening here?'

'He's fine, really fine, Lisa.'

'You do remember? Machine man beaten by a broom? He tripped over. Him. He should have known those beers were there without looking. He ... he collapsed, Leon. And then all this?'

Her voice trailed off. In the silence, Leon pulled the top off the beer, emptied it into his glass. He took hold of Lisa's hand. She looked up, aghast.

'What's happening?'

'He's fine. He's neo; you know he can't be anything but fine.'

She let her gaze drift from Leon's face to his shoulder, to a point far behind the wall of the room.

'You know I wouldn't lie. Do you want another beer?'

He flipped off the top and passed over the bottle. She took it and dribbled the beer into the glass. They both watched the pale gold stream and the froth climbing up the side of the glass. When she spoke, it was low and even.

'Leon, I have known Ben for ... a lot of years. I've been married to him for the great majority of them. It's not your standard marriage, but as far as it will ever be possible, I know him inside out. Over these years, I've been ill plenty of times, laid up in bed with head colds, chest colds; broken bones; infections; you name it, if a woman could, then I did. But in all these years, when I've been coughing, sneezing, having fevers, Ben's body has never been an issue. He's still young, they're not the same as us—he's got another thirty-five years at the minimum. Yet tonight, something happened. How come falling over hurt him?'

Leon's silence alarmed her.

'And what were you two laughing at?'

'Eh? something Kirsty was doing before we left. Look. Don't you and Ben ever talk about things?'

'Of course we do.'

'I know you joke about it, but don't you ever talk about him? What the two of you are doing together?'

There was a silence. He looked down at the table, tracing the grain with his finger as he waited. When she spoke, she had to work hard to keep calm.

'When we came down here, all those years ago, it was because we thought people round here wouldn't mind. You off-grid types didn't have restrictions, zones, licences, all that crap. And no race riots—not that type, anyway.'

Leon laughed. 'People are pretty cool, but as a couple, you're not exactly part of the wallpaper. I never knew how you two could be so naïve as to think that Ben could get away with it. Why didn't you stay up there in the city? At least he could have landed a job. Didn't you realise no-one would touch you two down here? At least up there he could have made some money.'

'You think it's bad round here? You should have seen us in the old days. Cities are neurotic. Half the time the energy's feeding you; "Ben's neo, sick!" And half the time that same energy's tearing you down. The aggression could be incredible. They served people steak at every party. And I mean people steak.'

'Oh, come on!'

'I tell you, the final straw, the thing that made us actually up and leave, was a party. A mixed-type party down along Collingwood Street. Back when it was all OK. Good evening up till then. Ben and I were so much in love, it scared me. We were all in this enormous loft, four, five times the size of this kitchen. Then there was the roof. Flat, with a low balcony. The way up was by a ladder. It was in the back of the kitchen downstairs. Hard to find. That's what saved us.'

'From what?'

'At the time there were gangs running all around having a load of old-fashioned fun, just a-burning and destroying. Some of them were religious, some of them were political. That night, we got a bunch who had a grudge against people like Ben. They were prepared to take it out on anyone who looked like they had done without a mother. And their friends. A lot of people got injured; quite a few of them died. Ben and I decided we'd rather not be round there anymore. So here we are.'

She fell silent for a minute or two.

'Anyway, I thought you knew all that. You mean Ben never told you?'

'He never talks about the city,' said Leon.

'So now I'm going to stop being side-tracked and you are going to tell me what's going on here tonight.'

He summoned courage.

'I'm talking about you two as a couple.'

'What do you mean "As a couple"?'

'I don't want to spell this out, but—'

'We're both sixty plus, and I look it and Ben doesn't. So what? You think it's not nice? What we do at bedtime? You think he should go down the beach and grab a nice neo-girl? Screw you.'

'Lisa, I don't think anybody should leave anybody. I don't know a better suited couple. But that's not the issue.'

'Well, what is?'

He hesitated.

'Ben told me once that you wouldn't ever talk about him, the real low-level him. What he's made of. How he works, moves, thinks. Sure, you joke about it all the time, and you seem really tight, the two of you, but he said he spent years trying to get you to discuss this. Then he gave up, thought, maybe you were right, and it didn't matter.'

'So Ben's a machine and I'm insensitive and I don't let him pour his silicon heart out any time he feels like it. What's that got to do with him lying up there in bed?'

'Neither of you is facing it. Ben isn't human, and he never will be, no matter how much you both paper over the cracks. But he isn't unusual anymore. We know a lot more. The fact is...'

His mouth was dry. But he had to go on.

'You're old, getting older, and Ben hasn't even begun. You mentioned he's got years left. That's true. He's facing another century, minimum. He'll get ageing problems, spare part glitches, like what happened tonight, but he's going to go on and on. Out of all the thousands of artificials operational, there isn't one that stopped from old age. No one knows what their real life-expectancy is. Even the early prototypes, the crudest lab models, look like they spend their time working out and eating vitamins. A full-blown system like Ben—well, who knows?'

'What has that got to do with tonight? What has that got to do with you? And what the hell has that got to do with anything?'

She stood up, grating her chair back over the brick floor.

'I've known Ben since we were both younger than you and don't you tell me he's a 'system'. Do you think we don't know all this? So what if we don't talk about it? So what if we don't invite the neighbours round for cake and self-discovery? That's because we don't bloody well have to.'

'I'm sorry.'

She rubbed her eyes. Tipped her bottle into the sink. Leon studied the tabletop. Carried on.

'I don't think you should be worried about Ben. The reason that Ben wanted to take this trip over to the islands wasn't only to see Kirsty and everybody. Sometimes—I think he feels you're too...'

'What?'

'Just because Ben still looks like he's in his twenties doesn't mean that he thinks like that. Sometimes I think you should lay off him a little.'

' "Lay off him." '

'Come on, Lisa, you know you can be jealous. Give him a chance. There are two things he tells me, time after time. One: he doesn't have a clue how long he's got left. Two: he is totally, stupidly in love with you. So stop doubting him.'

He waited.

'I should keep my mouth shut. I'm sorry.'

She still wouldn't look at him.

'I'm going up to bed. Don't worry about Ben; he's a lot stronger than we'll ever be.'

'Maybe you're right. It's OK Leon. I'm tired.'

He waited, but there was no more.

'See you tomorrow.'

He gave her a small smile, then closed the door behind himself.

Lisa listened to his footsteps recede up the stairs, then a pause, until he flushed the cistern. Tears formed in her eyes. She walked out onto the veranda and looked out over the road to the beach.

The sea was beautiful. She stood there for a time. Memories of the loft party she had told Leon about ran through her head. It was one of the few truly horrific things she had experienced in her life. She could still, forty years later, feel the strength of the inhumanity expressed that one night.

The raised voices and the music from downstairs didn't impinge on the conversation in the different corners of the darkened roof. Someone over on her left was smoking. She stood on the small wall around the edge of the roof, looking at the busy street fifty feet below. She swayed, feeling drunk, but before she had time to call him, Ben's arms came round her waist, steadying and holding. She was used to being surprised by him; would she ever get used to the things he could do?

She turned to fall into his arms, and he laughed. They kissed, and over his shoulder she saw Garric's head emerging from the trapdoor that led to the downstairs. There was something wrong with his face. She kissed Ben again but with losing concentration; there was definitely something wrong with Garric's face. She looked back and saw him collapse in slow motion, gripping one of the rusty old satellite bowls cemented into the roof. People gathered round him, one by one, in the same dreary slow motion. Then someone started screaming.

The crowd moved apart for a second; she saw bleeding

from the side of his head. He convulsed on the floor, blood flowing grey and free in the half light.

She turned to Ben to find he was no longer at her side. She had heard him swear a moment or two before when the screaming started. She turned back to the trapdoor to see him climbing down fast, shouting something to some unseen person, lit by a harsh red glare from the room below.

By the time they let her downstairs, they had turned the overhead floods on. They had wrapped the dead in refuse sacks, neo and real alike. Nearly all the surviving partygoers had left. The ones that were remaining talked in low voices in the kitchen amid the remains of the food. Two bodies lay, still uncovered, near the rope swing in the centre of the massive attic. They had remained untouched, she supposed, because of the amount of bleeding they had done from their wounds. There was still a panic about blood-to-blood toxicity in those days.

People jolt with fear as the door to the attic burst open. Ben came in, carrying a bundle of black polythene. He wrestled with each body, slipping in the mess underfoot, panting as he lifted, once slipping to fall across the half-covered figure he held in both arms. As he struggled and swore, the humans in the kitchen came out and formed a circle around him. They said nothing because there was nothing to say. They watched as his feet and his knees created a nervous pattern of coagulating blood on the boards of the attic floor.

He didn't let her sleep with him that night because they weren't sure that all they had washed the blood off. They talked past daybreak. Two days later, they were married by a non-too fussy registrar. Then they had left town.

In the countless revisits to that party Lisa had made over the years, she had long since found the key to the whole thing. It was not the violence, or the deaths that had offended, it was the attitude of the people there to the bodies—and to the blood. Not long before the party, she had been in a bar on her own. One neo, a big evil-looking one, had been talking to a crowd of reals, said too much and a fight had started. He had stamped all over them, claimed self-defence when the police arrived, and got most of the reals in the place arrested. Lisa still remembered what he had said that had caused the fight; they had been talking about the new epidemic that was slaughtering the old people across the city. Newcastle was still hauling itself away from the lymph flu, so this was none too smart. Then, getting louder, he had announced that everyone knew human blood was no good. Too many infections. It was getting tired, wearing out. Then there was the fight.

She had been foolish, she knew, to have ever believed that Ben's special power could transfer to her. She was only human, but he was the next thing along the line, the next evolutionary stop. He didn't age. He was bright, and new and would continue to be until very near his end, whenever that would be. If that would be.

In the bright moonlight, the sea before her was an animate thing, reflecting the bank of grey cloud above. It was the colour of pearl, flat and smooth, a sheen on its skin as it lapped at the sand, separated from the world Lisa was in by the thin barrier of dark beachside foliage. She let herself down the steps and walked on down towards the thin strip of sand, pale silver, half glimpsed through the dark undergrowth. She paused in the centre of the copse of trees.

There, on a bush, was a single flower. Dark, arterial red; edges blackened, but blooming still under the canopy of the dark needles.

Here among the cypress trees, it was almost dark.

There were thorns in the undergrowth. The land had grown black. The only thing that was light was the sea. The moon lit a cold, flaming path stretching away in front of her. Bright, mysterious, molten silver mirroring the night sky, a contrast with the black of the earth.

Up above her, back in the house, Ben lay in bed. He was sleepy, enjoying the unfamiliar sensation of bodily pain while it lasted. In his half-awake state, he still felt the familiar fear of being around Lisa. The 40 years they had spent together, the slow, unstoppable build-up of love between them, did nothing to soften the shock of the years' toll on her body. Almost as he watched, her skin loosened, her flesh softened, her hair thinned—and as she fell away from him, he chased her.

With all the superabundance of his eternal youth, he pursued her. He gave her desperate measures of laughter, excitement, love, and constancy, but nothing helped. With all the fire at his disposal, he held on to her, held her close, but still she slipped into the abyss. Rage had no effect. Pity was worse than that. It helped to talk to Leon—all friends were a help—but Leon was only 26. Ben felt the gap of experience. Many old men had young friends, so that uneven type of relationship could work. Experience and decrepitude ranged against ignorance and vitality, somewhere producing a balance.

But Ben was 65 now and growing older. What would happen when he was 90? Or 120? Could a man who had walked for 150 years even speak the same language as humans? Deep down, he knew there could be no competition.

He saw the retreat into his own kind as inevitable. He was calm, for he knew himself to be part of a new beginning.

He lay still, drowsy, on the verge of sleep, yet, as

always, aware. Aware of the room, the house, the earth beneath. Aware of the feel of the sheet on his skin, of the mattress under him. Aware of the flickering network of light in his brain. Most of all, aware of the man-made heart beating at the centre of his being. The heart that pumped youth and strength around his body. The heart that would never age. The heart that beat an unquench-able rhythm that now, he understood, could never be stopped.

EPILOGUE

2023 is the year I turn 60. That's quite a thing, and I'm not the first to be amazed by the number of seasons that lie behind me.

I was such a slow writer when I started. Whether it was fear, lack of technique, or whether I was too busy living to write, two years was not unusual for a single story, and some took me much longer. I'm much faster now.

These six stories come out of those first seasons. I wrote them a very long time ago, and they deal with old ghosts, but I had to publish them. I know they won't leave me alone until I do.

Writers never seem to explain where they get their ideas, and it's a question that always interests me. For those who share that fascination, here are are some of the places that these stories began. The seeds of each story.

THIS IS THE WOLF RUN

When I was ten, there was a burst of horror. Comics, TV shows, films, even toy shops, brimmed over with vampires, mummies, werewolves, skeletons, and their ilk. Models of Lon Chaney as the Phantom of the Opera, and Boris

Karloff as Frankenstein's monster, would leer at me from my bookshelf. Peter Cushing and Christopher Lee battled constantly in Transylvania and an old-fashioned England. American men were trapped in sub-atomic worlds or walked with the heads of bluebottles. Witches and aliens jostled to abduct me during the evenings, and Dracula tapped at my window all night.

Amidst all this I plotted with a similarly obsessed friend. Bruised and driven by this world of Hammer Horror, we thought about creating a real-life werewolf experience for a hapless friend. We weren't stupid, or malevolent, enough to carry it out, for which I'm profoundly grateful. However, guilt is a powerful thing, and the fact that I'd even had this idea haunted me for seventeen years, until 1990, when I could no longer resist making a coded confession. I sank into Ray Bradbury's *October Country* and began.

I took our childish wolf prank, blended it with Kate Bush's *Hounds of Love* ('it's in the trees, it's coming!') and from there came memories of *Night of the Demon* and the idea of passing runes written on a piece of paper to summon a demon.

The story works out one conclusion of giving too many dark stories to fresh and impressionable minds.

THE ICE SEED

I began this properly in the spring of 1990, had it finished by the end of 1991. It stands alone, in that I don't know and can't see where 99% of it came from. It therefore could be the most 'original' writing I've ever done.

The things I do know are clear.

I was half awake on an early morning commute when I saw Berkhamsted Castle in the mist. An image dropped into my mind: an old man smoking a pipe while sitting in an alcove in an ancient wall. The alcove and the wall above the man was stained with decades of pipe smoke. It was all part of a ruined castle, which the man had grown old looking after. Something about him spending his life in one place in the world appealed to me when my own life was so unsettled.

I'd had the phrase 'a pale-skinned boy with sea-green eyes' knocking around since the summer of 1987.

The phrase 'Our father had a steamboat' just popped out in 1990. I don't know why.

When I was a student a friend lived in high up in one of those deck-access concrete crescents in Hulme. His flat was all cement walls and steel industrial furniture, but he had a little cat he called John. I liked that.

Beyond that, this story is not from me. Some other force took over while I wrote it. Getting it down on paper was a process of slowly (always slowly) writing down a gift from some unknown outside agency. I'd say that agency was God, but the story doesn't contain much of his character, so that can't be right.

CALENTURE

This began in 1987, inspired by footage of the Challenger disaster I saw in the IMAX cinema in Bradford that summer. I added my admiration for the Ray Bradbury short story *Rocket Summer*, in which a father stops mowing the lawn to watch his son's rocket pass overhead on the first manned mission to Mars.

I didn't finish this one properly until 1994, when I was working as a technical author. It wasn't the best of times, and I think that explains the bleakness in the story. Writing manuals for IBM mainframes could be a grim business, and the days were often long, dry, and low on emotion. I found myself typing non-IBM words like 'green', 'grass' and 'sunlight' just to feel something. I'd put the words up on screen, and watch them for a while, before deleting them and going back to 'process', 'batch job', 'console' and 'print queue'.

That wasn't enough, and I turned more and more to my own world. I'd sit close to my screen so no-one else in the office could see what I was actually writing and escape into my short stories. One day I found myself back in the early 80s, absorbed in memories of a holiday in a remote village in southern France. I realised that, if I changed one or two things about this time, tangled up the relationships a bit, invented a few new desires and generally made things messier, then the holiday could belong in *Calenture*.

INDIAN SUMMER

This began in pine trees, sand dunes and the Atlantic. It was the summer of 1982. I was 19, and I was sweltering in a tent near the beach at Soulac-sur-Mer in south west France. I'd hitchhiked down there at the end of June, and been there for weeks, swimming, hanging out with the campsite workers, enjoying the sense of nothing to do and a big wide world before my first year at university.

The evening before I'd heard three people had died swimming off that same coast that same summer. I loved the beach, being out in the world for the first time, and I especially loved swimming in the sea. That three people had drowned nearby at practically the same time seemed bizarre. Eerie even.

I tried to write what I felt. A strange image came to mind: a man walking across a field of maize. The maize was high and blotted out the horizon as it waved in the wind. The man seemed to walk in a bubble, alone, against a big sky. I couldn't make sense of it all, or what I was trying to do. I stopped writing, went for a swim, forgot about it all.

Four years later, when I wrote a story for a competition, I picked up this image, and kneaded it and pushed and poked it out, until more and more stuff came. The ruined town by the sea was a a memory of wandering through Boulogne Sur Mer in November 1981. I was very proud of how the hissing of the rain in the last paragraph referenced the snake from the Garden of Eden. Clever, that, I thought.

Gollancz published *Indian Summer* in 1987, which undeniable fact propped me up over the next eight years when I couldn't sell a bean.

OLD PERSISTENT SPIRITS

It was 1989. I was 26, and I lived in Milton Keynes and had a new job at a software company in Harrow on the Hill. After only six months I knew I was in the wrong career. I would use the ninety-minute commute to escape into the main event: writing. One morning I saw a strange, undersea world. There was a giant fish moving down there too. I wrote that up for a while then stalled. I didn't know what came next.

Then I remembered the golden skeleton with ruby joints, which I'd found in a strange book called *Loop* in a bookshop in the East Village in Manhattan in 1986. *Loop: 50 Ideas for Pictures* was by a writer called Peter Zabelskis. It collected of images, seeds for short stories, given to anyone who cared to pick them up. I still have it. (Thanks Peter if you're out there. I've read *Loop* many times.)

Beyond that, one of my friends had joined the Royal

Navy after college and while I blundered around in computing, not knowing how to become a writer, he'd just got on with things and was already an officer. His story of a shark-infested 'hands to bathe' in the Caribbean interested me. (As did the word 'calenture'.)

I borrowed the title from a line in a Comsats Angels song and fans will already have realised that. The Comsats were about the best band ever. A few of us thought that, and probably all still do. (Hi, Mark, Charlie and Pete.)

It was only in preparing this book for release in May 2023 that I realised this story had one more influence. This seed has been under the surface for over thirty years without me noticing: Bob Dylan's song *Isis*, on his album *Desire*. That album has obsessed me since the late 1970s, and *Isis* is all about grave-robbing, a yearning for a distant woman, and pyramids 'all embedded in ice'.

IN THE DAYS OF INCREASING AUTOMATION

Looking at this story, written over 35 years ago, I'm surprised to see how what I thought was deep fantasy has become ordinary. Covid; pandemics; personal relationships between humans and AIs. None of it any good.

In August 1986 we were on a Trailways coach, going from New York to New Orleans. The road ran along a coast road, past a forest somewhere on the very edge of Louisiana. I saw isolated wooden houses, nestling in the trees by a great expanse of open water, and then I felt (rather than heard) the sound of a church bell. It was hot, clammy, and we had been travelling for thirty hours on the same bus. I was very much in love and the world was a gigantic adventure. We were just starting out. I wondered what this image of the house meant; why it felt so significant, and sombre.

We stood and looked down from a high, dangerous, roof, but it was the George and Dragon pub on St John Street in Clerkenwell in London. We went to the attic party, in 1986, but it was in the lower East Side in Manhattan, not Newcastle in the UK. There was indeed a rope swing, which I thought was cool, but there were no fights, and no-one died. The stone angel was in Camden, South Carolina. Our coach stopped there for an hour, and we wandered round a stonemason's yard in the heat.

Back in Manchester in 1987 I read yet another Bradbury short story, *Gotcha!* I absorbed the ideas of the absolute unknowability of your lover, and how old age and the death of love are implicit even in those first moments of a new romance. The story scared me, and moved me, and made me want to write against it. So, I did. I notice my story doesn't fix the problem.

I found the proper solution many years later when I discovered the Holy Trinity. Because of which I can say that, even in these worrisome days of truly increasing automation, I have even greater faith in love.

DO YOU WRITE TOO?

I write all kinds of things: SF, crime, drama, police stories, magical realism, Christian fiction, radio plays, TV scripts. I'm keen on voices that we don't hear too often these days.

And Yet is my publishing imprint. I call it that because we live in a fallen, sometimes very broken world, and yet amid all that there is always hope.

I would like to publish more new writing from kindred spirits. If that's you, look at www.andyet.live and drop me a line.

Phil Gladwin